BLOODLINES

Published in the United States by
Beckham Publications Group, Inc.
P.O. Box 4066, Silver Spring, MD 20914

ISBN: 978-0-9816505-9-3

BLOODLINES

A novel

Donald T. Beldock

THE Beckham
PUBLICATIONS GROUP, INC.

Silver Spring

For Lucy,
with whom everything is possible

NARRATOR'S NOTE

I'm writing this to get it all straight in my own mind. I'm not sure anyone else will have a chance to read it because I'm under professional constraints I'd have to weigh carefully before I ever let that happen. So I'm going to tell part of this story as I saw it, lived it, and actually know it happened, as much as anybody can do that, with a good deal of reimagining, so many years later.

I have never kept a personal journal or a diary, except for tracking billable time. And that limitation will have me re-creating some conversations as if word for word, with as much accuracy as I can muster, and summarizing others where I can recall the sense but not the syntax.

Nonetheless, Danny, I have to warn you, was quintessentially a private person, even as an adolescent, keeping his own counsel, playing his own games, and, to me, at least, always revealing of himself only what he chose to at any given time. So if my account raises more questions than it answers about what was going on in his mind while these events unfolded, I can only tell you, I'm still in the dark there, too.

The other part of this story I spent a lot of time and investigative effort piecing together from multiple sources. It's as accurate as I can make it without having firsthand knowledge of much of it. So I tell it in TPO. When we're through here, I think you'll agree it's really all one long story told in two voices, as it should be.

Peter Cowen, 5/2/12

CONTENTS

DANNY '90 I

I DIDN'T HAVE A PRAYER, BUT I WENT BACK TO THE JUDGE ON the very remote chance that he had reconsidered my representing Miller. He was firm. He had talked with a few key partners, and one was apparently sympathetic to my misgivings. But the consensus was clear: Miller had the same rights as any other potential client, essentially, to his day in court with the best representation we could give him. And if his idea of that entitlement meant me, that's what the firm would give him. Then he added that he would officially take the second chair. Full stop.

I called Moynihan the next morning and was put right through.

"I was just about to call you, buddy boy. We're out of time. It's now or never," he said as soon as he got on the line, leaving me about as much wiggle room as the judge did.

"My only option is to resign, and I'm not ready to do that."

"I hope you don't make your case to the jury any better than you did to your partners."

"What's the timing look like?"

"Now that you're officially opposing counsel, I don't think I should tell you."

"I am officially engaged at this time, but cut the chickenshit."

"Already pregnant, huh? OK. Here's your one and only break: we're ready to go to the grand jury yesterday. Don't say I never gave you anything."

"Thanks. That's sporting. And in the same spirit, I just want to tell you I'm wishing you luck."

"Prick. You know I'm going to need it."

"And you know I'd a helluva lot rather be with you."

"Me too. But it is what it is. See you in court, Counselor." And he rang off.

It was as if the lines had been tapped. McGuiness called me within the hour to tell me he and his client wanted to see me at my office right away. I set the meeting for 2:00 p.m. in one of our conference rooms and lined up Judge Farkas and a senior associate. It was no surprise to me that both of them cancelled other appointments to make this one.

Everyone was on time. I made the introductions. We shook hands and sat down. McGuiness said they had reason to believe the U.S. Attorney was about to go to the grand jury seeking his indictment on multiple counts of federal securities law violations. He said that they had not met with him or his client, but Danny had been notified by mail that he might be the subject of an investigation.

"Do you have any idea what it's all about?" I asked both of them.

"I believe it's a fishing expedition," the lawyer said.

"If they don't have something substantive, it would be very uncharacteristic of that office to ask the grand jury to indict and probably a serious tactical error," I told them and then turned to the judge. "Wouldn't you say so?" essentially rhetorically.

"I'd tend to think so, but it depends on what they have, of course," he answered, looking at me but clearly addressing the table.

Danny answered this time. "I don't believe they could have anything of consequence. I play by the rules." He paused, and then went on after flipping his fingers against his right thumb. "They could have trumped-up something, forced some guy they can squeeze to fabricate a story that serves their purpose in return for 'leniency.' But we ought to be able to knock it down if they have."

"Danny, I'm sure you've been told you can't have a lawyer representing you before the grand jury."

"I don't need a lawyer to advise me on how to tell the truth."

"Well," I said, "that's a good general rule to follow. But it's not always that simple. In complicated situations, even the truth has to be managed carefully to avoid misunderstanding. Grand juries, on balance, tend to believe federal prosecutors. That's the essence of the old saw about the DA and the ham sandwich I'm sure—"

"Many times, Peter," Danny interrupted. "But I'm sure you know how to prevent that in this instance."

"Again, I have to tell you, it really depends on what they have."

"I'm telling you, there's nothing for them to have."

"Perhaps not as you see it, Danny. But there are some facts I want to be sure you have in mind when you speak with that kind of assurance."

"Such as, Counselor?"

"Let's start with your legendary trading record."

"I'm a damn good trader, without a doubt. Not necessarily any better than Stern or Mnuchin or Greenberg or Burke, but certainly very good. Maybe as good as anyone around. And so far as I know, that's no crime."

"I didn't say it was. I just think you should recognize that the scale and the consistency of your success tend to raise suspicions."

"Understood. Not everybody loves a winner. Most people do, but not everybody. And I am a winner, most of the time . . ."

"An astonishing percentage of the time," I said.

"The day I find out that's a crime, I'm out of this business."

"That's the result we're being asked to help you avoid, as I understand it."

"If that's the real issue, I'm ready to take it all the way to the Supreme Court. And I'm not going to lose in the end. The economic system we've created over centuries requires markets, and markets require trading, and trades are zero sum, producing a loser and a winner almost all the time. There's no rule against winning most of the time."

"Well, trading may be a zero-sum game, but the justice system isn't. We get a lot of split decisions and virtual draws. But that's another issue we'll have to face in court, if we get there. Nevertheless, there is a presumption against the extraordinarily consistent winner, which doesn't help your cause.

"And there is another factor that has probably drawn invidious attention to you from regulators and prosecutors. You've become a celebrity, and there's another active market in stories, true and false alike, about celebrities. You presumably know that the market in Danny Boy stories is very active. And you should know, if by any chance you don't, that the U.S. Attorney's office pays as much attention to some of them as a good trader does to the tape."

"Even the bullshit," he said.

"Bullshit and Gospel, probably in equal measure, Danny, because in the final analysis, they don't really know until they investigate."

"What a waste of time and money."

"They would call it, as I did when I worked their side, 'vigilant surveillance' essential to the credibility and proper function of markets."

"My ass," he snarled.

". . . is at risk, I'm afraid. That's the way it is."

The judge summed up. "Peter said justice was not a zero-sum game, Mr. Miller. But he never said it was not adversarial in the extreme." Then he turned to me. "So if you will excuse my interrupting unbidden with a suggestion, I think it would be wise if Mr. Miller and his counsel told us whatever stories might be bruited about that could be construed adversely to Mr. Miller's interests in the subject proceedings."

McGuiness didn't answer immediately, and Danny appeared to be waiting for some signal from him. It seemed both of them were aware of at least some "stories" that qualified and thinking through whether it made sense to cough them up. The judge glanced at me, and I broke the silence by telling them that whatever they were hesitating to tell us, somebody else already knew, and their failing to give us the information would only impede our ability to defend Miller when, and if, as was likely, whatever it was emerged in discovery or on trial.

McGuiness said he wanted to have a few minutes with his client alone. We both thought, without even having to check with each other orally, that private discussion made sense, and McGuiness would probably press Miller to bring up now anything that might prove embarrassing so we wouldn't be blindsided. I asked the receptionist to find an empty conference room for them and send someone to escort them to it, which she did immediately, and they went off together.

The judge and I each returned some calls while the clients were out conferring, then we speculated about what kinds of revelations we might hear. Neither of us expected anything momentous, but we were hoping McGuiness could coax Miller into telling us anything we should know. When they were out for almost an hour, we gradually began to revise our expectations more pessimistically, until the judge said, just before they returned, "Something's up, Peter, and it isn't good. But I suggest we don't react, no matter what we hear. Just try to tease it out gradually if we have them talking. We need to get everything we can while we can, or at least as much as possible before they clam up."

Right after that, the receptionist called in to say they were ready to resume our meeting, and then brought them in again as we requested. When they entered, I tried to assess what the jury would see if Danny testified. A very good-looking, meticulously groomed young man of about thirty, a touch less than middle height, fit, poised, perhaps a bit too confident, and something of a dandy in his very British, dark gray serge bespoke suit, nearly horizontal spread collared, striped shirt, light lavender satin necktie, half-Windsor knotted and loosely gathered purple and black foulard silk pocket square.

I concluded, just as they were taking their original places at the table, Danny crossing one leg over the other and sitting back in the chair with his hands folded in his lap, that he was likely to be perceived by a typically class diverse New York jury as an impressive, rich, probably very successful fellow, but not very likeable.

McGuiness exhibited some tension before he spoke, keeping his hands out of sight. "As you must know," he began, "in Mr. Miller's position, people regularly approach him with offers to give him information that they represent to be of special value."

My prosecutor's gut told me something important was coming.

"What kind of information might that be?" I asked, very mildly.

"Of varying levels of importance," McGuiness said, "frequently regarding or potentially affecting public companies. Occasionally, information not generally known to the public."

"This information comes to your client unsolicited?" I asked

"Characteristically."

"Mr. Miller is, of course, aware of the regulations applicable to the exchange and use of 'insider information,'" I said. "How does he protect himself against the misuse of such information?"

"By himself?"

"Let's try that question first," I suggested.

"He advises me that he is extremely careful not to misuse it."

"Meaning?"

"That he never trades on it."

"Personally, that is."

"That is my understanding."

I directed my next question to the client. "How many traders work for you, Mr. Miller?"

"It's still Danny to you, Peter," Miller answered.

"Fine. How many, Danny, directly and indirectly?"

"There are about twenty traders in my firm."

"All under your direction?"

"No."

"Really? Who provides their trading capital?"

"The firm."

"Your firm?"

"Yes."

"Which pays their compensation."

"In a way."

"What does that mean?"

"We provide them trading capital, and they share in gains and losses on their trades, so if they're successful, they build up personal stakes in the capital they're using to trade. In that sense, they're also working for themselves while they're working for the firm."

"Do you control their trading activities?"

"In most instances, no."

"But in some instances?"

"I would not say we control their trades, other than to keep an eye on their capital positions, where they stand with their positions."

"How frequently?"

"That varies."

"Would it be fair to say continuously?"

"In dollars and cents."

"Let's start there," I said. "Dollars and cents, net long and short, at any given moment."

"We have a pretty good idea."

"At all times."

"If our risk managers are doing their jobs."

"Of course. Would you say those risk managers tend to be doing their jobs at all times?"

"They do, or they don't last with us very long."

"Let's go back to those people who are always trying to provide you with valuable information."

"Yes."

"Do you ever accept that information?"

"That depends on the source."

"Do you ever trade on that information?"

"No."

"Directly or indirectly?"

"What does that mean?"

I did not look at the judge or McGuiness. Straight at Miller. "Everything anybody says in this room today is attorney-client privileged communication. It can't be discovered. And it can't be used against you. But there are facts at issue that can be determined by other investigative means. Then those facts can be introduced in evidence and used against you. So if you'll stop pussyfooting and tell us straight-out whether you've obtained and used inside information, directly or indirectly, for your own benefit, we stand at least a fighting chance of designing a plausible defense for you against charges relating to that activity.

"But if all you're going to do is play rope-a-dope with us, you're wasting our time and your money and probably heading for the can."

"Temper, temper, Counselor. Remember, the customer is always right," he came back to me, unflapped.

"Not in this store, Danny. We're not in your business. We charge big fees. With the judge, me, and our associate, the combined rate is over $1,300 an hour. But we pride ourselves on giving honest value.

If we don't or we can't, we don't take the money. We don't play your 'beat the sucker' zero-sum games here. So talk straight with us or walk out."

McGuiness adopted injured dignity. "You have no right to speak to my client that way, Mr. Cowen."

"Not if he's only yours, Counselor. But if has any intention of having me represent him, I'm going to tell it like it is. And if he doesn't like it, take him home."

I expected the judge to try to lower the temperature, but he didn't. He just looked out over his horn-rims, firmly expressionless.

McGuiness stood and placed a hand on his client's shoulder. Miller sat still, looking me right back in the eye. Then he said softly to McGuiness, "Sit down, Michael, please. We have business to do here, and I'm going to do it, whatever nonsense my old classmate puts on, for whatever his reasons. I'm used to his righteous indignation number, and it doesn't faze me."

"Level with us or walk, Danny. My next question is, what consideration do you give for the inside information you get and trade on? And the next one after that is, what makes you think that one of your informants is singing to the U.S. Attorney?"

"Who says I think that?"

"I do, because you wouldn't be here if your only worries were some possible violations of proposed proxy rules that don't even have the force of law yet. You're here because you think you're in very big trouble, and for some reason, you're convinced the judge and I are the only lawyers who can save your ass this time."

"And that's also a crime, Mr. Prosecutor?"

"No, it's not, per se. And I'm not the prosecutor, as you very well know and ought to be damned happy about. But if you try the same bullshit in the courtroom you tried here, you'll see a prosecutor who can turn that into perjury, sure as Bob's your uncle, and that, glamour boy, is a felony."

"I didn't have to go to law school to know I can't be forced to give any testimony that might tend to incriminate me. Or have they rescinded the Fifth Amendment while I wasn't looking?"

"Right you are. You can plead the Fifth instead of incriminating yourself or perjuring yourself. And the SEC can pull your ticket, too, just to make sure you don't set a precedent."

"I can live with that."

"I might even be able to get you that deal if you want to plead right now. The U.S. Attorney might like that precedent."

"No, thanks, Mr. Avenging Angel. I'll just get myself the best lawyers money can buy, beat the charges, and clear my name."

"We're really flattered, Danny. But if you want the best performance your money can buy from this set of lawyers, you'd better tell us everything you know and everything you're worried about. Even then, we can't give you any guarantees. Without that information, as I've been telling you, you're wasting your money."

McGuiness revived. "Mr. Miller does not have total recall, and he's a very busy man. How can he possibly be expected to remember everything he's ever been told and by whom and when?"

"First of all," I said, "we're not asking for everything he's ever heard, unless, by any chance, he's made a habit of recording it all, in which case, of course, we'll want to hear that or see the transcript. What we absolutely do need is an account of any inside information he has ever solicited, paid for in any form, and either passed along or traded on or directed or permitted anyone in his organization to trade on."

McGuiness said again, "If the investigation were to lead to an indictment and a trial, you would, of course, get all the information leading to any such allegations prior to trial."

The judge decided to handle that assertion, beginning with a question. "Counselor, have you ever tried a criminal case?"

McGuiness said that was not his field.

The judge said, "I take it your answer is no."

McGuiness said he practiced corporate law, exclusively.

The judge said, "Therefore, it is not surprising that you apparently have such a misguided understanding of how the processes operate in this arena."

"If my limitations are relevant, please be good enough to tell us how."

"I won't presume to take on that assignment, Counselor. Suffice it to say the U.S. Attorney's office plays hardball, and federal judges, despite their genuine commitment to impartiality and the principle that the accused is innocent until proved guilty, tend to give them a fair amount of leeway to make their cases."

"Given the experience from which you speak, Judge, I'd be most interested in learning how that practice is likely to affect this case, if it should come to trial."

"I think it is fair to say that information available to the prosecution is not invariably volunteered in full by the prosecution to the defense prior to its emergence in the courtroom. Since the rules of practice do dictate that it should, I wish I could tell you that those rules are always meticulously observed. But I'm afraid I must, sadly, inform you that anything can happen in a trial, and surprise is not uncommon."

Then I added, "Which is among the most compelling reasons why it behooves your client to tell us everything he knows before we ever get to trial. Nothing is more damaging to a defense than a lawyer taken by surprise in the courtroom. That's why we keep pressing the issue with you."

"Then I think I should make my position very clear," Danny said firmly and calmly. "I do not intend to say, now or at any other time, in this room or in any other, anything which I believe might be construed in such a manner as to tend to incriminate me. Are we all clear on that, gentlemen?"

The judge leaned in over the conference table. "That's your legal right, certainly. But it's ours to decide if we accept or decline the representation."

"Judge," Danny said mildly, "with all due respect, you and Peter wouldn't be here meeting with us now if that issue hadn't already been decided by the firm."

"That is a reversible decision," the judge said, less mildly.

"Well," Danny answered, "unless or until it is, can we move along here? Time is money. Lots of money, in this case."

DANNY '74

WE MET IN THE LATE SUMMER OF 1974, JUST BEFORE THE BEGINNING of the school year. I thought the circumstances were unusual then, to say the least, and that's why I remember the whole day so clearly. Looking back, I see them as pretty much standard for the Millers. My mother had gotten a call a couple of days earlier from the headmaster, Dr. Thacker, explaining that there was a new boy from Chicago starting with us in the fall, that he knew no one in the school, but that he was supposed to be a good tennis player and a top-level wrestler. He had competed and done well in local boys' and juniors' tennis tournaments, and he was an All-State wrestler in Illinois as a sophomore.

The headmaster thought it would be a good thing to do for the school if I would call the new guy and invite him to play tennis before the semester began. After some discussion with my mother, I did call him at the Long Island number Dr. Thacker provided. I gave my name and asked for him, introduced myself, and welcomed him to New York and the school. Then I suggested we get together to play some tennis.

He thanked me for my welcome and said he would love to play with me. He suggested I come out to his house in Oyster Bay where they had a court and a swimming pool. When I told him I couldn't drive in the city yet, he suggested I take the Long Island Railroad, which he understood, came from Midtown Manhattan right out to Oyster Bay. He said he knew there was a train that got in around 11:00 on weekdays and that he would pick me up at the station.

21

I told him I'd be on it the next day, and I was, dressed in pressed chinos, button-down, rep tie, and blazer (after a little more discussion with my mother), carrying my tennis clothes and rackets in a canvas satchel I used for team travel.

The train trip took less than an hour, making a lot of stops, and I arrived at the Oyster Bay station just before 11:00. When I stepped out of the railroad car and headed for the ramp, I saw at the bottom an average-size kid about my own age in tennis clothes, waiting alongside a wood-paneled station wagon, next to a man shorter than he in a tweed jacket and cap.

"Peter," the kid called out and trotted halfway up the ramp to shake my hand. He took my satchel, and said, "I'm Danny Miller. It's good to meet you."

"Good to meet you," I said. "I'm surprised you recognized me."

"You were the only one getting off the 11:00 o'clock who looked like the tall blond kid named Cowen in the tennis team picture," which meant he'd checked the yearbook. Reasonably clever.

That exchange got us off to a fair start. He introduced me to the little man he called John McGriff, and we settled into the wagon, Danny in front and I in back. While we turned out of the car park onto a tree-lined street Danny called downtown Oyster Bay and on into a residential neighborhood, he kept up a steady stream of one-sided conversation.

"I don't have my license here yet either so Johnny has to drive me around, which he doesn't really appreciate doing, and I always sit in front to avoid pissing him off any more than necessary."

"It's not the driving I mind, wherever you sit. It's just spoiled rich kids that rile me."

As Danny kept rattling on, I looked out the window and watched the houses quickly grow larger as we headed what I guessed was north. We turned on to a lane completely overarched with trees. The houses were mostly blocked from view by big hedges and brick and stone fences, but I could occasionally glimpse through a break in the barrier, as we drove slowly by huge homes with broad lawns glistening green in the sun and seeming to run on down to the Sound.

We pulled into a gated driveway and rolled up a gravel road to one of the bigger houses I'd seen, with a tall columned portico and connected structures stretching what appeared to be over a hundred feet wide and on down behind to the water spreading out to the horizon like a swath of silver silk.

"Villa Miller," Danny said, stretching his arms wide across the vista.

"It's magnificent," I said.

"I don't know about that," Danny shrugged. "But it'll look good, I can tell you, because my mom is in charge of the makeover."

"Makeover?"

"Oh, yes. Come on in, and I'll show you." He strode to the door, opened it, and stood back to let me pass inside.

There were workmen everywhere, on ladders, on the floor, on tarpaulins strewn over every visible surface and enough obstruction to make it difficult to get a sense of the downstairs except to register that the rooms were large, high-ceilinged, and airy, brilliant in the midday sun.

"Come back in two weeks, and you won't recognize the place. My mom does this everywhere, top to bottom in a month. You could say it's her business, except that she doesn't take on any other clients these days."

Then, "Come on, let's get down to the pool house so we can get you changed and go hit some. You'll meet the dazzling Dorothy at lunch."

Dorothy, I took it, was his mother, but I was feeling a little embarrassed about being so overawed and didn't want to ask any unnecessary questions. We walked out through the painters, plasterers, carpenters, and helpers, through French doors at the back of the house, and onto a broad patio with a lot of floral patterned cushions on what I knew was white-painted wrought iron and wicker furniture, then down a path through a formal-looking garden to the pool house.

It was big enough to accommodate my family, and framed one end of the pool, which seemed to run right into the Sound, although it must have been twenty feet above the little beach below. Danny led me into a small bedroom and dropped my bag on a chair.

"Why don't you get changed and meet me over at the courts?" he said and waved to his right as he walked back out of the pool house.

"Courts, it is, uh-uh," I said to myself, getting just a bit irritated with the splendors of Villa Miller. I changed quickly and followed the direction of his wave. Another long segment of that lawn stretched out ahead of me, and, about fifty yards away, up against a stand of tall trees, I saw two tennis courts side by side, with the trees on one flank and a low green anchor fence on the other. As I approached I saw that there was another small white building on the near left side of the courts and a table set under a big umbrella a few feet away from it. Leaning against the fence I saw a big young man who looked like a college guy and an older man about Danny's size, all in whites and looking very comfortable around the courts. One of the courts was Har-Tru; the other one closely cropped grass.

Danny introduced us. The big guy had played number 1 for Princeton that year and was off to law school in another two weeks. His name was Carl something. The man was the pro at Sands Point Country Club.

The pro's name was Phil Martel, and I thought I'd heard of him as a big-time doubles player before I was born. He asked me with an easy smile what surface I liked. I told him both, but maybe grass today because I didn't get enough chance to practice on it.

He suggested that he and Danny, as the little guys, play the big guys, the Princeton fellow and me. We flipped a racquet. The Princeton guy won and chose serve. We shook hands and wished each other luck. The pro put his arm around Danny's shoulder and talked softly to him as they walked to their choice of side, which didn't matter much with the sun near its zenith.

We played three tough sets in an hour and a half. Carl and I each had big serves (which was why I chose grass), and he was very good. Smooth, fast, heavy topspin from both sides and court savvy. Danny was smooth, too, and very quick. It looked as if he had played a lot in good competition, and the match was on serve the first few games.

The most impressive thing to me was the pro's game. He didn't seem to run much, but he was always in the right spot in open court and at the net. He always hit the ball just hard enough on great angles. Danny was struggling with both of our serves, but the pro took them on the rise unless we went up the T or way wide, and he returned for as many winners as we hit. They both got their first serves in and placed the ball well, with enough pace, and we couldn't get much going against them either.

Then with me serving at 4-4, the pro moved way in from the baseline and started to chip his returns short, soft, and just over the net, the way my father did playing me singles. I wasn't slow, but I didn't get off the mark too quickly. He had me straining to get to the short ball and flipping it up when I did. He or Danny knocked off the setup volleys, and at deuce, I hit a wide second serve that Danny whistled down the line for a winner. At ad-out the pro chipped one that squirted just over the net into the alley and, *bingo*, we're down a break. Danny held for the first set.

And that's the way it went though the three sets. They played just a little better than we did each time, and we lost by a break each time. I don't think that Danny made six mistakes in the three sets, and I don't remember the pro making one.

We shook hands and exchanged congratulations, and Danny led us over to the umbrella table where I noticed sandwiches and iced tea already laid out. Before we sat down, I followed Danny's gaze up the lawn and saw what appeared to be a young woman in a big straw hat and white pants walking along a diagonal path toward the table. When she reached us, Danny introduced me and said that Carl and the pro were old friends of his mom, with which they happily agreed.

Over lunch, Mrs. Miller, in a deep, musical voice I pegged as contralto, told me how lovely she thought it was that I had come out to visit and that I was to "come often and always feel welcome" in their home. She looked like someone out of *The Philadelphia Story* to me, and I couldn't believe how beautiful she was, smiling and looking directly into my eyes. I realized up close that her hair was blond under that big brim and that her eyes were a lustrous brown and huge. Her scent almost dizzied me with its blend of the garden and the sea. In thirty seconds, I was in love and overwhelmed. "Yes, ma'am," and "No, ma'am" were about all I could manage as she questioned me gently between laughing exchanges with the other three.

"Danny, I like your new friend," she said when we had finished the sandwiches and the pitcher of iced tea, and some huge, stemmed strawberries dusted with sugar and placed near the center of the table for hand-picking. Then to me, "You be sure to say good-bye before you leave, and promise me we'll see a great deal of you."

I managed, "Yes, ma'am," again and stood to clear her chair back as she left the table.

"You have lovely manners", she said, smiling into my eyes as she stepped away.

I blushed and managed one more "Thank you, ma'am," and watched her start back on the path again heading up and across the lawn to the house. Very pretty girls always got to me quickly, and I had already had at least three crushes, but the impact of Mrs. Miller on me was way beyond any of that.

"She'll make it up there OK," Danny laughed.

I turned back to the table, blushing, I imagined, and said, "Your mother sure is beautiful," before I could check myself.

"She certainly is," Martel agreed, and the college guy said, "Amen."

"Let's play a couple of more sets," Danny suggested. "You play with the old pro this time."

We went back out again and played two more close sets. Martel played just as well as necessary to win 3 and 4, and I held up my end. Then, after we exchanged "good play, nice tennis," all around, Martel, with a big smile and iron handshake, said, "You've already got a fine game, Peter, and you can only get better. If your singles is as good as I think it is, you and Danny are going to win a lot of matches for that school of yours and for a long time after you've left the place. Your coach is a lucky fellow, and you're a splendid young man."

I thanked him, wished the big guy well at law school, and then headed up with Danny to change at the pool house. I showered in one of the oversized tiled showers and passed up the steam room.

We were dressed, Danny in chinos and an Izod Polo shirt, and out in fifteen minutes. Danny said we just had time to catch the 4:24 if we hurried. We walked back through the house, quiet now, with all the trades gone for the day. I asked if I could say good-bye to his mother, and Danny said he would do it for me because she was probably taking a nap, as she usually did in the afternoon.

"But don't worry, she liked you a lot. You passed all the initial screening," he said.

Just as we came out the front door, Johnny materialized with the wagon, and we took off for the station, arriving just in time to catch my train. I told Danny how much I had enjoyed the day and thanked him. He thanked me for coming out and suggested we try to play once more before school started. We agreed to talk by phone and set it up.

On the train, which appeared to make most of the stops on the way back to Penn Station, I tried to get a handle on the day and the Millers. I hadn't really learned anything about them, other than what was right on the surface, but that impressed me by itself. My overriding observation was that Mrs. Miller was the most beautiful woman I had ever seen, in or out of the movies. Next, I was almost as impressed by the way she had set up the day, somehow finding out from the headmaster which kid could help her son starting out in a new private school in a new city, getting Thacker to reach out to my mother, inviting me out to their gorgeous estate, and making me feel a bit as if they were doing me a favor having me there and "approving me." They were obviously socially adept, or at least one of them was, and the other very confident.

It doesn't take too much to make a presentable guy, who has at least one good sport and can take a joke, fit in at a new school. Give him one boy who's with the "in" group to sponsor him and maybe recruit one more "A-lister" to join him in the lead, and the new guy is made, in with the right people overnight. Danny would have me, if the Miller plan worked, and I wouldn't have any trouble getting him a cosponsor.

Another reasonable observation from the surface was that the Millers were rich, because they not only lived on a pretty grand estate in very fancy country but also, if I had picked up the quick reference properly during the chatter around the courts, they had a co-op apartment on Fifth Avenue where they were going to live, at least during the week, while Danny was at school. And, whatever else Johnny may have had to do around the estate, he certainly had enough time on his hands to be available to drive on a moment's notice when needed. Then I remembered that I had seen a man and a woman, both in uniform, setting the table near the courts and clearing it after lunch.

All in all, the two Millers I had met lived a pretty opulent life, had some real clout, and knew how to use it smoothly. None of these observations, I soon learned, were off the mark, and my general assessment understated the case to a substantial degree.

As for Danny, himself, he was a very good tennis player, seemed to be an OK little guy, quick-witted and good-looking, if a bit of a "wiseass", too. He shouldn't have any real trouble making the grade at Horace Mann, I thought, provided he didn't play "rich kid" too much. Of course, we already had some over-the-top rich kids at the school who managed all right fitting in, so maybe even that might not hurt his social prospects with the boys. And it surely wouldn't hurt him with the girls.

When I got home, my mother was in and asked me about the day. I gave her a brief report, leaving out most of the details on Mrs. Miller.

"Is she nice?" my mother asked.

"I guess so," was my considered response.

"Well, if he's a nice boy, I hope you'll help him get off to a good start with the kids at school."

"Yes, Mom, I think that's what it was all about."

"I guess that's quite true, Peter, but I know you will do all you can to help him. And you won't forget to write a note, will you? You know it's always best to send it right away."

"Sure," I said, "but I'll have to get her first name or his dad's."

She sat right down at her desk and wrote out Mrs. Benjamin Miller's full name and their Oyster Bay address for me.

Danny and I did play once more before school, this time singles on the red clay courts at Riverdale. Smiling John, as Danny called him when he was not around, drove him in and back from Oyster Bay. I won the match, but barely, two out of three sets, and we sat on the empty spectators' stands to eat the picnic lunch my mother had prepared. He was talkative and affable. I spoke a lot less, but agreeably, and we were comfortable with each other by the end of the afternoon.

Just a week later, school opened, and I came in excited, as I always did in the fall, anxious to get into action after a dull summer as a day camp counselor in Westport. My friends were all at least a little excited, and I was standing around with five of them who had been my best buddies before Danny arrived. We had no single leader because all of the boys were honor-roll students, varsity athletes, BMOCs. But there was a subtle rank order generally accepted within the group. Big Robby Mazer was the top gun. He punched me in the shoulder and said he was glad to see me. Robby was almost as tall as I and thirty pounds heavier, fullback handsome, and already comfortable in the aura of varsity football star-in-the-making. I caught sight of Danny over Mazer's shoulder and waved him over.

"I want you to meet this new guy. Robby Mazer, meet Danny Miller. Danny's my friend from Chicago, and he's going to win us lot of tennis matches playing number two singles until he knocks me off the ladder, and we're going to play doubles together, if I can get coach to agree. I hear he's also a pretty good midfielder."

They shook hands while I continued the long introduction, ". . . and this big moose plays a little fullback and first base. Which is fine with me because it keeps him out of tennis competition, and he's no pushover."

We all laughed, and Robby punched Danny in the shoulder. That was it. Everyone who mattered saw that exchange right outside the Fifth Form homeroom, and Danny was "in" from that moment on.

He stayed pretty close to me those first few weeks, kept his wisecracks under wraps until he had established friendships of his own, and never, in my hearing, let anybody know about his family's money or social position. Of course, some of the kids were savvy enough to put together the house in Oyster Bay, the Fifth Avenue apartment, and the little guy with the station wagon who met him on a corner three blocks away from school most days. But there were plenty of kids from two—and three-home families in the classy areas and even more who could arrange to get a ride to or from school if they wanted it.

Within a few weeks he knew everybody in the class and most of my friends in the classes above and below as well. We competed for the tennis ladder, and I held my place at the top. Danny came in third, behind the senior John Carstairs, who was the captain. Everyone knew Danny would keep challenging Carstairs until he nailed him, and then keep coming after me, but we kidded between ourselves about it.

He also made the soccer team as a starting midfielder, and I was given the chance to start as goalie. We had all but one of our classes together and spent almost the whole day, every day, sitting, standing, or running within a few feet of each other. I think we both enjoyed it; I know I did. And I rarely thought about how "naturally" the Miller plan had worked out. It looked as if it just happened by chance.

Danny joined the Drama Club and immediately began getting parts in the plays. I tried out for the Glee Club and made it (as I hadn't the year before when my voice still cracked). And we both took the school bus to Harlem once a week to tutor smart kids up there. So we didn't have much spare time for sitting around and talking, but when we could, we usually did that together, too. Sometimes we were alone, more often with my other friends, who were rapidly becoming his, too.

I was very impressed with him, gliding into full stride in the school so smoothly and quickly. I wanted to know more about him, especially what he was thinking, but that wasn't easy.

"Danny," I remember saying one day when we were alone for a few minutes during an open hour between classes, "we're going so fast during the day that—I don't know about you—but I hardly ever get a chance to think about anything. Except at night, after I get my work done, I sometimes have a little time. Then I do think about different things. Do you?"

"Not much."

"But when you do, what do you think about?"

"Not much."

"You don't think about anything?"

"Not really. I kind of play it by ear."

"Why do you think that is?"

"I don't know. I never considered it. What do you think about?"

I was about to start telling him when some of the other guys came into the empty dining hall and sat down at our table. We abandoned the inquiry.

Of course, he had to know that he'd made it from "new boy" to the top echelon in record time, but he never explicitly discussed it. The closest he came to bringing up the subject was a casual remark that he was "lucky to know me from day one." Accomplished in several areas, and "regular guys," we gradually became the informal leaders of our group and the class, by an uncontested consensus, without diminishing Robbie's stature as the toughest guy.

Danny and I grew steadily closer as junior year went on, gradually becoming a little unit within the clique. We studied together, went to most of our classes together, and spent a lot of our spare time on weekends together. We were also playing soccer together, so for that season and the tennis in the spring, we went to practices together, too. The only time we weren't paired was in the winter when he wrestled, and I played basketball. But even then, we were both working on the newspaper together.

The friendship added its own dimension of enjoyment to what was generally a very happy time in my life, and the competition between us in almost everything kept us both working hard and well at whatever we did.

I had just started dating a girl I met in Westport at the end of the summer. She lived right around the corner from me in Manhattan and was a senior at Brearley. This fact suggested that the romance, if any, would be a very brief one. It would take more independence than I thought, Julie Bregman had to date a boy her age and a year behind her at school, once the scene switched to Manhattan. But I was working up one of my crushes and wanted to keep the relationship going as long as I could.

Danny knew no girls in Manhattan, so on my second or third date in town with Julie, I'd asked her if I could bring him along to meet her, and she had agreed.

We went to the Bregman apartment on Seventy-fifth and Park, arriving about 7:00 p.m. Julie met us at the door, and I introduced them. She led us from the marble-floored entrance hall into the paneled library, and I could see Danny catching a look through the open connecting door into the big and very elegantly furnished living room. We were just sitting down on the facing caramel colored leather couches when a girl even taller than Julie, and just as pretty, walked in through the door we had entered.

"This is my big sister, Diana," Julie said, and then introduced us as we shook hands. "She goes back to Smith tomorrow, the lucky stiff."

"Oh, I wouldn't mind having my senior year in Manhattan again," Diana smiled. "It was the best year of my whole life."

We talked a few minutes about how much fun her senior year at Brearley had been, and then I asked Julie if she would like to see the Paul Newman movie at the Beekman. She agreed, and I was just about to do the right thing by asking Diana if she'd care to join us when Danny beat me to it.

"How would you like to make it a foursome?" he asked as if it were the most natural thing in the world.

Danny, I was thinking, *you've got to be kidding. She's at least two years older and in college,* when Diana answered him, "Sure, why not? I can finish packing later."

It was obvious that both girls found Danny very attractive, with his dark hair and bright brown eyes, blunt, symmetrical features, and quick smile. I was a full head taller, with my father's long narrow face, sandy hair, straight, narrow nose, pale hazel eyes and serious air, and had never been called "cute" or handsome, to my knowledge.

And so, mix-matched as we were, off we went, Danny taking Diana's arm, I holding Julie's hand, and the four of us, but mostly Danny, chattering like old friends off to a party.

After the movie, we stopped for pizza, and then laughed our way back to the Bregmans' apartment. There was still no sign of the parents. Julie and I went into the library where we necked for about an hour. Danny and Diana went into the living room. What they did, I didn't know and don't to this day. But the double doors were still closed when I kissed Julie good night and walked home alone about midnight.

* * *

There were cultural sea changes taking place in those years, the first oil crisis, *Roe v. Wade,* women's rights, gay rights, impeachment, the Vietnam disaster, "hell no, I won't go," girls in the Ivies . . . Our group talked about them in and out of classrooms, sometimes with passion, but I took them much more seriously than Danny.

He was very interested in Wall Street, and that didn't particularly interest me, in those years. He still rooted for the Bears, Blackhawks, and White Sox; I was devoted to the Giants, Rangers, Knicks, and Yankees. So we talked sports more than politics or social issues, not much about the war, which seemed very remote. We did talk a good deal about girls, and a little about colleges.

"You really want to go to Yale?" Danny asked me one day.

I told him I always had and saw no reason to change.

"Did you ever think about a co-ed school like Stanford, or Harvard, where they have a lot of girls' schools around?"

I told him I hadn't and that I knew Yale guys who had cars got to Smith and Vassar, Conn College, and Sarah Lawrence pretty much whenever they wanted. I liked the idea of being close to New York, too. As the year went on, Danny began to grow more and more interested in Yale and said he liked the idea of our rooming together. By spring break, we were both settled on New Haven.

That year I played number one, the senior captain; Carstairs, played two; and Danny three most of the time, although the coach would switch the order for some opponents. We won eleven of our twelve dual matches and finished the season at the top of the independent school league. Our coach said he knew the Yale coaches and would put in a word for us.

Danny had been well prepared in his studies at his day school in the Chicago suburbs, and he had no trouble making the adjustment to ours, which he said was a little more demanding. We both lettered in our off-season sports and finished near the top of our class for the year. That performance set up a happy senior year, as well.

We both did well on the SATs, received our early decision acceptances from Yale, and won all of our matches for an undefeated tennis team. By the end of that year we were close as brothers, closer in my case because my younger brother was off in his own world, just about oblivious to me.

I had learned that Danny was fiercely competitive about everything and with everybody, but especially with me. We also had our differences in opinions and tastes. He was a natural Republican, identifying with the privileged without any hesitation or exception. I was already a liberal Democrat, pretty much aligned with my parents on major issues. I was intensely partisan about segregation and fervent about most social issues. Danny was laid-back. We rarely argued between ourselves, though, because he simply didn't care enough about matters outside his immediate scope.

I was not laid-back. I watched Danny glide through those two school years with awed fascination. He studied hard and made excellent grades, played his sports not only well, but consistently better. He made friends easily and quickly and by graduation was probably one of the most "popular" guys in the class. He made business manager of the newspaper, varsity club (with his three sports), the honor society, and senior prom co-chairman.

His first flash of celebrity had come in the late fall of junior year. Mr. Sklar, the wrestling coach, just before the beginning of that season, arranged to have an exhibition bout with him, open to see for anyone who wanted to watch. There was a pretty big crowd of kids in the upper school who decided they wanted to see the match, and a special kind of "big game" excitement had built up while we were sitting in the basketball stands waiting for Danny and the coach to come out of the locker room and start the match.

I didn't know a lot about wrestling, and had only watched Danny win a couple of bouts. with ease, evidently outclassing his opponents. But I did know Mr. Sklar was supposed to have gone very deep in the NCAA in the 145-pound class three years in a row as an undergraduate at Lehigh, reportedly winning the division as a senior, and he certainly still seemed to be in shape when we saw him around the gym. He looked much bigger and stronger than Danny, and I had always thought he talked pretty tough and probably was. The word from the wrestlers was that the 145 pounders, at Sklar's level, were considered the best NCAA's competitors, pound for pound, and I talked to Danny very seriously in the morning, telling him that I thought he ought to be extra careful because Sklar might have something to prove, even against a kid.

When they came out to set up on the mat, with the young assistant coach, really right out of college, as referee, Danny, even though he hadn't yet started for the season that wrestlers' drill of getting their weight as far down as they could to qualify for the lowest possible weight class, looked like a stringy muscled little kid who didn't belong on the mat with the much-bigger, by maybe twenty-five pounds of toned muscle, grown-man coach.

I have to say, again, that I knew very little about the sport, but seeing them next to each other on the mat, I was really worried that Danny could get injured. It just didn't look like a fair match. I did notice, though, as I never had before, that Danny, in short shorts and a cutaway sleeveless jersey, had exceptionally long arms for his size.

Then the ref started them, and Danny was moving so fast it was hard to follow him, incredible how quickly he darted and how little Sklar's weight and strength seemed to matter in the bout. Danny's swirling, sinewy arms consistently knocked the coach off balance for takedowns, and spinouts, his moves taking him out of Sklar's reach, and his own seeming to turn the coach' s weight on itself, setting up escapes and reversals and piling up points, as if he were giving a lesson.

The match was short, but Sklar was almost breathless and clearly beaten when it ended, with the coach first shaking Danny's hand, then lifting it into the air as he said, still breathing hard but with considerable grace, "Boys, you just saw a future Olympic Middleweight champion here today, and if Danny Miller puts on any more weight and muscle, without losing his speed, he'll be the undefeated NCAA 160 champion before he's old enough to shave every day. Take it from me, you'll be proud to tell your grandchildren you saw him wrestle, and you'd better catch his show every time he's on the mat.

"You're never going to see the likes of him again."

He finally dropped Danny's hand and tousled the kid's short hair with his own big-knuckled right.

As we were leaving the gym without the coaches, Billy Ackerman, the halfback and linebacker who had played ever minute of every varsity football game that fall as a junior, called out to Robby Mazer, "Hey, Big Robby, you want to take on this skinny shrimp from the boondocks with me, show him what we do to half-pints like him?"

"Sure," Robby said, "if we can get enough other big guys to help us. I'm not taking on that little monkey with just you on my side."

"So," I said to Danny on the way downtown, "how'd you like that, Champ?"

"More than I can tell you, buddy. Even you. It was great. From the first minute, when I realized how much he'd slowed up, that he could never really get his hands on me, except in starting positions, and then couldn't even hold on to me, I knew it was over. It was just sweet."

Danny was happy, no question about it. But he really didn't seem very excited, and certainly not surprised. I'm sure I was more impressed than he was.

*   *   *

Midway through senior year, I remember the headmaster walking up to us as we sat reading assignments in commons during a study hall period. The honor-roll boys didn't have to attend.

"Good morning, gentlemen," he said. "I see you're both hard at work." Then he pulled a chair around to the end of the refectory table we were flanking. "Don't let old Peter here make you too much of a grind, Danny. You've done a wonderful job at this school in every way. Now let's make sure you enjoy the rest of your time here. It goes all too fast." Then he turned to me. "You too, Peter. Make sure you have some fun."

"It's been great all the way, Mr. Thacker," said Danny, smooth as always. "We've been having a wonderful time, and the only thing we're worried about is college acceptances."

Thacker stood by us for a moment, rubbing his chin, apparently weighing whether to say something more. Then he placed both hands on the tabletop and said, very softly, "It's not very prudent for me to say so, fellows, because some strange things do happen in the admissions process, but I don't think there's one chance in ten that you two boys are not Yale freshmen next fall. So just forget about it and enjoy these final months here. And keep that under your hats."

He touched his index finger to his lips in the "mum's the word" signal, smiled, and walked away.

"That was kind of nice of him, wasn't it?" Danny said.

"I sure hope he knows what he's talking about. And I think we ought to finish this assignment, anyway, just in case."

"Loosen up, Cowen," Danny laughed. "He's too smart to say that if he didn't know something. He's like my extra grandfather, Duke, who never says anything he can't back up."

"Let's hope so," I said.

"Christ, Peter, we've got to build up your self-confidence a little," he smirked.

"Danny," I said, "you've got more than enough for both of us."

I was too locked onto the Yale prospect at the moment to follow up the "Duke" remark, and he brushed me off when I tried to come back to it later.

We were both admitted early at Yale, and the last few months of prep school were golden. The masters gave us a very easy rein, and we spent more time in "discussion groups" than in formal classroom settings. We still felt some urgency in competitive sports, but little about grades and class rank. Neither Danny nor I was seriously in the running for the Gordon Award to the top scholar, and we were both confident of cum laude and reasonably so about picking up one or two incidental academic honors out of the usual eight. It was a blissful interlude in my life, and, for a change, I cherished every happy moment of it.

MAX '21-'25

Sixteen-year-old Max Landsberg came to this country alone from Hamburg early in 1921, passing through immigration at Ellis Island. He had learned a little English from a professor of linguistics who was a fellow steerage passenger and used it to look up family friends, the Frankels, on Delancey Street.

They took him in until he could get a place of his own and helped him get a job making deliveries for a shirtwaist contractor operating in a loft on Orchard Street, where he set to work diligently to make something of himself. He also studied English at night with a neighborhood rabbi who helped immigrant boys get started "on the right foot."

The contractor's shop, the rabbi's little apartment, and the Frankels' home were safe enough, but the streets were very dangerous for Jewish kids whenever they wandered out of the few square blocks of their Lower East Side neighborhood. Even there, gangs of roving toughs, usually second-generation Irish or Italian, would rumble through to have some "fun" baiting and battering Jews, particularly kids alone or in small groups.

Most of the greenhorns were strictly fodder for the marauders. But a few of them, like Max, had learned to defend themselves, either in the old country or, through natural talent, very quickly on the streets of the new one. Max was not a big fellow, but he was a very tough kid and, if he got into a fight, usually hurt one of his adversaries enough to send a message.

Still, he generally "minded" his own business and kept out of trouble where possible, until one day he turned a corner and saw three of the toughs in a circle beating up two wailing boys in black hats, suits, and long curls. He ran into the circle, whacking one tough in the eye, kicking another in the kneecap, and then really working over the third one until he turned tail. He told the two cheder kids to run away and then began pummeling the two assailants still hunched over, nursing their wounds.

A couple of days later, while he was on the street delivering a stack of embroidered shirtwaist panels, he was stopped by a guy he knew to be a low-level mobster named Jimmy B., dressed in a tight-fitting suit, loud, striped shirt with a white collar and patterned tie, shined shoes, and a peaked cap. To Max, he looked snappy.

"You Landsberg?" Jimmy B. asked, and Max told him he was.

"We got some work for you that's easier than pushing garment racks," said the wiseguy.

"What kind of work is that? For who?" Max asked.

"For us. You know who we are, don't you? We can always use a smart kid who can handle himself to run errands, keep an eye out for us sometimes, and maybe collect something somebody owes us, once in a while."

"That doesn't sound too hard," said Max.

"Most of the time, it ain't," said Jimmy B.

"And what does a guy get paid on this job?" asked Max, and the wiseguy told him, "Ten bucks a week and found."

"Found?" asked Max to whom the ten was more than twice what he was making from the contractor.

"Yeah," said Jimmy B., "you know, a little extra here and there. It should at least double your take, averaged out."

"I have to think about it," said Max. "Where do I reach you?"

"Just ask at Kaplan's candy store," Jimmy B. told him, "but don't think too long. You got 'til tomorrow morning."

Max finished his day's work, returned "home," and asked Mr. Frankel what he thought.

"I think you should stay a hundred miles away from those *banditen!*" Frankel told him.

Max thought about it overnight, then told the Frankels in the morning that he was taking the new job and moving out. He left with a hug and a kiss from Mrs. Frankel and their little daughter, a handshake and an imprecation from Frankel.

"Don't hurt people for them," Frankel said.

"Sure," Max answered. "Not if I don't have to. And especially not our kind. Please don't worry, Mr. Frankel."

Max spent the next three years collecting for the mob and very rarely had to hurt anybody. Anyone he called on knew the threat he brought; no one wanted to find out if he'd really carry it out. As soon as he paid a visit, the debtor found the money, including the one-for-five-a-week standard interest, and Max delivered it dollar-for-dollar through Jimmy B. to the mob treasury.

By the end of the three years, Max was putting a little money of his own out on the street, with permission, and keeping a piece of the "vigorish." He was still living in a fifth-floor, cold-water walkup, but he was dressing like Jimmy B. and working on a plan to get other collectors working under him, with permission.

Then he had an "incident." One of his creditors fell behind on his payments and didn't respond to a low-key threat. In fact, when Max came back to the man's shoe store the next day, there was a hard guy waiting around, rhythmically smacking a cosh he held in his right hand into the palm of his left. Max appeared to ignore the hired muscle and addressed himself to the client.

"You've got it today like a good fellow, don't you?" he said to the little merchant, while idly picking up a low-top boot from a shelf along the wall.

"No," said the client. "Maybe next week business will be better."

The hard guy stepped a little closer, starting to edge between Max and the client, but before he could interpose himself, Max smashed the heel of the boot he was holding into the bridge of the hood's nose, which collapsed, spurting blood. Then he picked up the cosh the hard guy had dropped and whacked the client in the mouth with it. The effect was shattering and bloody as the client sank to the floor, whining and trying to staunch the bleeding from his mouth with his handkerchief, half-choking on broken teeth.

"Tonight," said Max. "You'll find me with all the money, tonight, or you won't be able to open the store for a long time."

The client and the hard guy stayed on the floor where they lay.

That night, the client didn't find Max, but the cops did, handcuffing him and taking him to be held overnight for arraignment the next morning on charges of assault and battery and extortion, "abey," in mob speak.

But after he was in the holding pen for less than an hour, he was pulled out for a bail hearing in night court. The magistrate set bail at $200. A lawyer appeared to post it with the court clerk, and Max was sleeping in his own bed by 11:00 p.m.

The arraignment was set for two days later. Max showed up at the courtroom at 10:00 a.m. as ordered. He met his lawyer for the first time. Somebody called the assemblage to "All rise." And they stood as the judge entered and sat alone at what Max was told was "the bench." Another lawyer asked for permission to "approach," which the judge granted him, and then said that the plaintiffs had declined to press charges.

The judge banged his gavel on the bench and called the courtroom to order. Max, whispering, asked his smooth-shaven lawyer what was happening, and the lawyer told him that it was all about nothing, his case was about to be dismissed, and Max could go home.

Then the judge said he wanted to address Mr. Landsberg. His lawyer told Max to stand up, face the judge, and look sad. Max complied.

"Young man," said the judge, "since one victim can't remember how he lost his teeth, and the other doesn't know how his nose was broken, and neither one can remember who hit him or if anyone threatened him, you are free to go at this time. But I advise you never to be brought into this courtroom again, because if I ever see you, or hear of you, in connection with a case like this, you can be sure you will not go home for a very long time." He then rapped his gavel again and said, "Case dismissed. Next case."

Max did not go home, but was met outside the courthouse by Jimmy B. who took him to the back room of a storefront office two blocks away. There they were ushered into the presence of a full-faced, curly-haired man in his thirties, dressed in a dark blue suit, white shirt, and small figured tie, sitting with his legs comfortably crossed behind an empty round table.

The man introduced himself as Michael Fine and said, "I know you're our tough little Jew boy, Max Landsberg." He did not offer Max or Jimmy B. a seat. "We like you, Maxey, and you could have a future with us. But the guy you messed up the other night at the shoe store is with another mob that's not so happy about you. Also, the judge meant business when he said he doesn't want to see you again. So we're going to suggest that you pack a valise and take a little train ride out West to a place where friends of ours will set you up, maybe in something new, and keep you busy for a while. We take care of good people, and even though you're not really one of us yet, you've made your bones, and we'll take care of you, too. Good luck to you and stay out of trouble."

Max thought that was pretty funny, coming from the source, but he kept a straight face and his mouth shut, except to say, "Thanks for everything, Mr. Fine." Then he left the back room and walked into the front with Jimmy B.

They stood at the bar, ordered two beers, and peeled themselves two hard-boiled eggs.

"What does all that mean, Jimmy?"

"It means you're moving to Illinois, Cicero Illinois."

Just at that moment, Max happened to be looking in the direction of the door to Fine's office in the backroom and he saw a widebody with his back to Max pull a revolver out of his hip holster, fling the door open, step in with the gun in his right hand, and swing his head around trying to find his target. Max took two long running strides, threw himself on the shooter's back, and managed to get his own right hand around the gunman's, still clutching the revolver with his index finger in the trigger ring. Fine was just coming out of the toilet when the gunman, stumbling, squeezed off a round into the floor, and Max landed two solid rabbit chops with his left hand to the back of the hit man's neck, while pulling him down by the gun hand and jumping up to stomp on it.

Jimmy B. piled on a second later and pistol-whipped the gunsel unconscious as Fine looked on smiling while he finished buttoning up his trousers. Max picked up the revolver by the barrel and placed it on Fine's desk.

"That's pretty classy work, Maxey," Fine said, offering his hand to shake. "I think you just saved my life."

Max, straightening his own tie, said, "I just happened to be in the right place at the right time, Mr. Fine."

"I'll say you did, kid, with your eyes open and plenty of nerve. I owe you, Maxey. If he catches me coming out of the crapper and gets that shot off straight, it's lights out for me. I won't forget this. We won't forget this."

Then he flicked his thumb at Jimmy B. and said, "Now have some of the boys take this creep downstairs and find out who sent him before they stuff him in the furnace."

* * *

Max arrived in Cicero with his suitcase full of "smart" clothes, a bank check for $2,500, and the names of two men who might be of some help to him getting started in the new town. Within a month, with a little help from his "friends," he owned a previously failing men's store on Washington in which he gave some back office space to a very active bookmaker known as Arnie Parlay.

Max bought some new merchandise on a credit line his friends arranged at the First Cicero Bank across the street and freshened the place up with a new coat of paint and some serviceable fixtures. Before long, a few of his new friends and some of their friends started coming into the shop and finding clothing they liked. A few months later, the shop, now called Max's Menswear, was prospering as its predecessor never had, and Max himself was becoming known in town as an up-and-coming young fellow. He devoted himself, when he wasn't attending to his menswear business, more to helping out his friends with the occasional difficult collection or go-between assignment than civic affairs, but he also began making more new friends at the local Democratic Club.

One evening, when he and his clerk were closing the shop, two hard-looking types in suits walked in waving handguns and told him they wanted what he had in the cash box. While the robbers were keeping their eyes on the front door and growling, "Get a move on,

Sheeny," and "Move it, Kike," over their shoulders to him, Max used his left hand to open the box he kept on the near side of the counter between himself and the holdup men and pulled a sawed-off shotgun from under the counter with his right.

Before they could register what he was doing, Max fired both barrels of buckshot into the legs of the nearest hoodlum, sending him screaming to the floor, and his partner, firing two wild shots behind him, out the front door and down the street on the dead run. Max picked up the gun the wounded man had dropped, and then asked the clerk to summon the police. They arrived in a few minutes, pulled Max off the hoodlum, scraped him up from the floor, and carried him out, telling Max to wait right there until they came back for his statement.

The next morning, two of the more senior of Max's friends came into the store and began to tease him as "Killer Landsberg." Then they gave him some serious advice.

"Max," the tall, older guy who was dressed like a banker said, "next time just give them the money, get a good description, and call us. We'll take care of the rough stuff." Then he produced a very earnest look and asked, "You got that?"

"I got it," said Max, looking equally serious. And that was the last time he ever touched a gun in his life.

DANNY '88-'89

IN SOME CIRCLES, MANHATTAN IS A SMALL TOWN. DANNY AND I would see each other two or three times a year whether we wanted to or not. After a while, I would exchange a cursory greeting with him to avoid imposing the tension on anyone else. But I rejected extended conversation with him, and he immediately accepted that constraint. Then the patterns of our lives intervened.

I had put in my year clerking for Judge Milan in the Second Circuit, and then five years as a prosecutor with the U.S. Attorney's office in Manhattan. I won a tax fraud case that got some publicity and an embezzlement case against a well-known executive which attracted even more attention. That press and my more standard credentials got me an offer to spend a year at Connolly, Dolan, and Farkas as a litigator in their corporate department, with a virtual guarantee of a partnership the following year.

Danny, I knew through mutual contacts, had gone from HBS to Goldman Sachs, where he quickly became a star risk arbitrageur and began making big money almost immediately. He was rumored to have brought several large personal and corporate accounts with him, and that advantageous circumstance was credited with giving him an early opportunity to shine he did not fail to exploit. He made a reputation as a brilliant trader and, after just four years on the desk, left to form his own firm, backed by some of his biggest clients. The word was that despite his jumping ship with those clients, he retained his relationships at Goldman.

He was said to have a position, sometimes two, in every big deal that was done in the '80s and to come out a winner on almost

45

every play. Those were very good years for Wall Street, and they were spectacular for Danny Miller, whose reputation for the Midas touch grew from deal to deal. The mythmakers said that he could tell whether a deal would make it to the finish line from the day the first block of stock traded and call the final price within five percent nine times out of ten.

Our divergent professional paths crossed during the year I was learning the ropes at Connelly, Dolan, and Farkas. One of the firm's trusts and estates partners called me into his office to meet a client who appeared to have a securities question. An arb was trying to gain control of the family company. The client, a grandson of the founder, was not involved in the business—although his brother was the CEO—and had been approached by the arb to sell his block of stock in a two-stage transaction. The client's name was Albert Walker III. The arb was Danny Miller.

Walker looked like a surfer in a good suit, blond, square-cut handsome, easy mannered, in his early thirties. "Miller's OK," he said. "I've known him for a few years. He says he likes the company and just wants to take a position. He's not interested in a takeover."

"An arbitrageur just happens to take a long-term investment position," I said.

The T&A partner either didn't pick up my irony or chose to ignore it.

"He said he doesn't want to run the price up because he may want to buy more. So he says he wants to buy half my stock and take an option on the other half, ten percent higher."

"What percentage of the company do you own directly?" I asked him.

"Including what the trust has?"

"Are you a trustee of the trust?" I asked him.

The partner answered for him, "No, he has no control over the trust."

"But it sounds as if he may . . . Excuse me, Mr. Walker. I mean, you may have a beneficial interest in what the trust owns. I will have to check that out."

"Anyway," Walker said, "I believe I own about five percent of the stock in my own name."

"About?" I asked.

"About," he repeated. "I don't know exactly."

"But you know how many shares you own?"

"Of course."

"Well," I said, "we can check it out easily enough."

"So can I sell him the stock?"

"On this limited information, it sounds likely, unless he's solicited too many other people."

"Good," Walker said. "See if you can work it out right away. I'm looking forward to telling my brother."

"We'll look into it immediately and get back to you as soon as we can," I assured him.

"ASAP," he said.

"Right," I said. "I'll be back to you through Arthur. But I may need more information, and I'm sure he knows where to reach you."

"Of course," said Arthur. Then we shook hands, and I went back to my office.

I could feel a meeting with Danny coming, and I didn't like the idea. I'd have been perfectly happy to let the next fifty years go by just exchanging the occasional perfunctory greeting with him. But I couldn't really tell Arthur I wouldn't advise his client. So I did the research that afternoon and found nothing clearly prohibiting the transaction, and since the modern proxy concepts were really just developing at the time, there was nothing that specifically opened it to question. As a prosecutor pressing to make a case, I might have stirred something up, but that wasn't my role anymore. As Walker's lawyer, I could bless it in good conscience.

I told Arthur that provided we got some representations from Danny, his client could make the deal on the sale and the option. He and the client were delighted. The client would pick up at least $10 million before federal long-term capital gain tax, and as a nominal Florida resident, would pay no state or city income tax on the sale. Not entirely incidentally, the firm would pick up an easy and substantial fee.

Barden called me at my desk the next day and said his client and Miller had made a deal and that he wanted me to start papering it up with Miller's lawyer that day. That morning I met Arthur, the client, and Danny, and his lawyer, in a conference room at Connelly. Danny's lawyer was a very bright and even more aggressive securities specialist named Michael McGuiness I knew from law school. I had an associate sitting in with me, and I expected him to do the drafting.

They all shook hands before spreading out around the conference table. Danny said it was nice to see me and asked how I had been. I thanked him, said I was fine, and steered the discussion to business. McGuiness was happy to get right down to work.

It took us less than half and hour to detail the terms and agree that we would prepare a draft to be ready for review the next morning. The clients were both delighted to have the matter moved along so quickly. Danny and McGuiness said they would review the contract as soon as they received it and that they would like to close by the end of the week. I asked McGuiness if his client could have good funds by that time, and both lawyer and client assured me that the money was accessible in a local bank account as we spoke.

We all shook hands again, and as Miller and McGuiness were leaving, I told them we would have the draft to them by early morning the next day and that I doubted there would be much reason for changes if we kept the deal as simple as possible. We could therefore reasonably expect to close that week.

When Miller and McGuiness had left, Barden said it was very important to close by Friday because Miller, whom he had seen I knew personally, had the reputation of being very impatient and probably had other potential sellers identified to jump to if this deal bogged down. I told him anything could happen in a deal, "as he well knew", but this one wouldn't founder because we were slow on the paperwork. He thanked me for that reassurance. I could see the associate getting tense, and I assured him we'd make it if I had to draft with him that night.

The closing went off as scheduled on Friday morning at eleven so Walker could deposit Danny's cashier's check for $10 million long before the banks closed. We all congratulated each other on getting the deal done so quickly, and Miller and his lawyer were apparently very happy, as well.

Arthur suggested that he, "his" client, and I have dinner together that evening to celebrate. I thanked him and demurred, citing a previous engagement without explaining that it was with my fiancée and some of her friends.

Danny had been agreeable and smoothly charming throughout the proceedings, and I felt that we had both managed to avoid revealing any sign of tension between us. Reading the unspoken signals, I thought I detected Danny taking some less than entirely wholesome pleasure in having delivered a low six-figure fee to Connelly for which I would get at least some credit.

*   *   *

It was more than a year before Danny and I ran into each other again. When we did, at a cocktail party in a penthouse on Central Park South, we exchanged the ritual pleasantries, and Danny attempted to extend the exchange, but I apologized and said I had to talk to another lawyer who was waiting for me, standing at the room-width living room windows looking out on the lights coming on up the fifty blocks of the park at dusk, in my book one of the most beautiful cityscapes in the world.

I walked over to the fellow, Jim Davidson, a partner in a top firm, and said over his shoulder, "What a sight, eh?"

"Incredible," he said, shaking his head in wonder.

We talked for a few minutes about a corporate case we had together. Then he brought up Danny.

"You know Miller?" he asked me. "I just saw you talking with him."

"We went to school together," I said, intending to leave it at that.

He pressed on, "Certainly is the Midas touch man right now, isn't he?"

"So I hear," I said.

"Started with nothing. Made his fortune from scratch in record time."

"Did he ?" I nodded.

"I have an extraordinary opportunity for him, really exceptional. Will you introduce us?" Davidson asked.

"For your sake," I said, "I really don't think that would be the best way to go. Why don't you have our hostess introduce you? Carole Mayer's an expert at that. She gives parties like this just to put people together. I'm sure she' be happy to oblige."

"Ah, yes," he said, shrugged off his disappointment in me, and set off to locate Mayer.

Angled into the room, I could see the steady flow of guests greeting Danny as they entered, most of them gathering in a rough circle of increasing circumference as they stayed within earshot of him. A good many of them, I knew to be "serious players," but with few exceptions, none among the women, they seemed to be in a state of barely controlled excitement as they stood around him, responding a beat too soon to any remark he made, any little laugh line he dropped, any gesture of inclusion he made.

As far as I knew, Miller was not designated as a special guest, but in that room of energized, ambitious, socially polished, successful men and women and their consorts, Danny Miller was the ranking presence. Thirty-one (and three months, to be precise, as I knew), just under middle height, trim, handsome, poised, elegant, and impeccably dressed (maybe a bit too stylishly by my father's and my own J. Press standards), Danny dominated, apparently effortlessly.

My drink tasted sour. I wanted to leave the party and head home. Then Julie entered from the foyer, smiled ruefully as she skirted the crowd around Danny, and crossed the room, arms outstretched to me, and kissed me on the mouth.

"God, Peter, where the hell have you been? Why don't I ever see you? Don't you love me, anymore?"

I held her at arm's length, produced my best smile, and confessed, "Always have. Always will."

"Then why?"

"It's a long story. But you know all of it."

"Peter, you're the man, the real man. Any woman with any sense would know that. He's all flash and light and the star fuckers can't resist him, any more than I could. But one of these days . . . poof, just like that, he'll burn out. I know, believe me; I knew, and I know."

"But that made no difference then, and it certainly doesn't now. He's what he is, and any man in this room would change places with him if he could."

"No, Peter. You wouldn't."

"I think you underrate him. He's very good at what he does, being Danny Boy, that is. And there are certain consolations that go with the job."

"But do they really matter?"

"One does."

"Which one?"

"You."

"Wrong, Peter. I don't go with the franchise. I'm a free agent."

I took her left hand in my right and raised the ring finger with the enormous diamond solitaire covering her first knuckle.

"Is it true what they say?"

"That diamonds are forever? No, it isn't. And they're not a girl's best friend either."

"If you're trying to get me to overcome my scruples and forget my grudges, it's working."

"Right here, right now? No. I am telling you that nothing is forever. You ought to know that."

"I should, all right."

"That's not what I meant . . ."

And there was Danny, behind her, sliding his arms around her bare shoulders, grinning, claiming possession, looking me square in the eye.

"And what are you two up to? A la recherche . . ."

"Ah, Danny," I said. "Got it in one, as usual. Reminiscence. Old times. Not your game, Danny. You live in the moment."

"Well, I'd better keep my eye on the prize, wouldn't you say, Counselor? There's always somebody trying to take it away, isn't there?"

I smiled mirthlessly at them, nodded, and turned back to the room, just as my wife swept into view with an attractive couple who lived in our apartment building. As the ladies exchanged air kisses and the fellows shook hands, Audrey apologized for being late and asked me to thank our neighbors for bringing her over in their taxi.

"I'd still be waiting if they hadn't taken pity on me. It's an impossible night," she said and blew them another kiss.

Just at that moment there was a shriek of laughter from the group around Danny, and we all turned to see him beaming at the crowd response to what was apparently something taken for witty that he had said. They were still laughing when the four of us began to walk through the party together.

Audrey, holding my outer arm, half-whispered to me, "Isn't that Danny Miller?" She squeezed my arm with both of her hands and her words tumbled together in a rush.

"The very man," I said, "but you've seen him before."

"I don't remember. Was he always that good looking?"

"A lot of money and a little fame have a way of making a man look very attractive," I said, as evenly as I could.

From then on, the annals of Danny Miller were so ubiquitously chronicled that hardly a month went by without a wide circulation newspaper or magazine story on him. I did my best to ignore them, but I found myself keeping up with his exploits, real and rumored. I generally skimmed the stories, looking for anything derogatory. It was hard to find in that confetti shower of adulation.

Hoping for Danny's fall did not take up much of my time or energy. It was only a little incidental dissonance in my life. The partnership was offered as promised and accepted with pleasure, and my share of the firm's profits gave me three times what I had been making as a prosecutor. Audrey and I had two kids in rapid succession, and together, our family unit took most of what little free time I had. I did play tennis once during the week at night and once on the weekends with buddies who were quality players. I began some involvement in Democratic politics, first at the state and federal levels, and later on the local scene. Judge Milan, for whom I had clerked, pushed me a bit toward his own allegiances and several of my partners made clear that they thought I had a general obligation to be as much of a mover and shaker as I could. It was the life I had hoped for, filling every waking moment for me, and the fullness of it satisfied me through those striving years.

MAX '26

MAX LIVED TWO BLOCKS AWAY FROM HIS STORE. ONE NIGHT WHEN he had just returned home from a few beers with his friends, he heard the fire wagons clattering by on Williams Street. Feeling a bit of premonition, he put his shoes and overcoat back on and headed back to the store. No sooner was he on the street than he felt the concern in his gut change to dread.

By the time he got to the corner he could see from down the block that flames were ripping though his store and overwhelming the two wagonloads of firemen trying to pump a weak stream of water onto the blaze with no visible effect. In the time it took him to walk the last block, the fire had engulfed the building and was tearing into the two on either side of it. The one further from the corner contained an upstairs apartment, and the ousted family, all of them, it appeared, were huddling together on the opposite sidewalk, watching their home disappear. He knew them all by sight and had spoken with the two kids on the street.

He walked as close to the fire as he could, then stood watching his life collapse in the flames. One fire crew moved their wagon over to the house fourth in from the corner and turned what was left of their water stream on the wall between the third and the fourth. They were hand cranking a pump that seemed to be pulling the last of the water out of the big barrel on one wagon while a second crew tried to hook up another unit that had just arrived.

The fire chief, whom he had met before, walked away from the wagons and over to him. In his helmet and black coat the chief stood over seven feet tall, towering over Max, his red-veined nose and cheeks shining in the firelight. "It's a great shame, isn't it, Goldberg?" he said grimacing in the heat of the blaze. "But there appears to be no loss of life. Thank the Lord."

"How do we know that?" Max asked.

"The family says they're all accounted for."

"That's good, at least," Max said, trying to look more relieved than he felt.

"It's a good thing for you, too, Goldberg."

"For everybody. Losing the businesses and the properties is terrible as it is . . ." Max answered.

"There'll be enough questions asked without any dead bodies," the chief said commandingly. "We'll want to know how the fire started and if anyone could profit from it."

"Yes, we will, won't we?" Max said expressionlessly. "And Chief, the name is Landsberg, the same as it was before the fire."

"Is it now? I'll try to remember that." The chief walked away to the nearer fire wagon.

Max watched until it was clear that the fire would not make it to the fourth building, and then he walked up to be family still standing in the street and asked them if he could put them up in his little apartment for the night. The mother thanked him warily and told him they would stay with her mother just a few blocks down the street.

He began to walk home slowly, thinking about how he was going to recover from the disaster. Exhausted, angry, depressed, he wondered if it was worth trying to put the business back together again. He owed money to the vendors for a good part of his merchandise and most of the fixtures, and after settling up with them he'd be starting over with less capital than he began with a year earlier.

He turned around before he reached his apartment and headed back down Clark Street toward the speakeasy where he had his beers earlier in the evening. The place was clearly wide open for business, no guard, no peephole, no sign of Prohibition. He just walked in, sat at the bar in his overcoat, ordered two Canadian whiskeys in succession, and did not share his troubles with the bartender. After half an hour of sitting alone, he decided not to bother with dinner.

He slept fitfully, waking several times in the night, and got out of bed the next morning at his usual five o'clock, feeling more angry than depressed. He knew damn well that the chief suspected him of setting the fire himself. That suspicion infuriated him. But he also knew that he had no insurance on the business, nothing to do with the disaster, nothing to gain, and everything to lose from it. But he believed it was no accident, and therefore, someone had started it.

The main thought on his mind that morning was to find out who did and why. He walked over to the little insurance agency where the local boss kept a cubbyhole office. Carlo Marchetti sat behind his desk and waved Max to the one chair in front of it.

"I heard about your troubles, Max," the boss said gravely. "I'm sorry."

"Thanks. You didn't happen to hear about how it started, did you, Mr. Marchetti?"

"We are looking into that," said Marchetti.

"When you learn something, Mr. Marchetti, will you let me know?"

"Yeah," he paused. "Are you broke?"

"Worse," said Max. "I have some cash in the bank, but I owe a lot more on the merchandise and the fixtures."

"How much insurance you got?"

"None."

"Yeah, we'll look into that, too," said Marchetti. "You'll hear from us."

"I'm going to have some time on my hands until I get back on my feet," Max ventured. "If there's anything I can do for you, will you let me know that, too?"

"Yeah, we'll let you know."

Max excused himself and left, wondering, as he walked out into the street, what all the "looking into" really meant and what he was going to do with himself now that he didn't have work to do, for the first time that he could remember. He had been working, at least part-time, since he was six years old, in Danzig, and he knew he'd have to get some kind of action going before long. He wasn't anxious to go back to collecting or running bets, but he knew he'd have to take what came, for the moment.

The next day, Max was sitting in a booth at the diner two blocks from what had been his store having coffee and a sweet roll for breakfast and reading the sports section of the *Tribune* when an out-of-uniform fireman slipped into the booth and sat down opposite him.

"The boss wants to see you, Goldberg," the fireman said without preamble.

"It's Landsberg," said Max, evenly.

"You can tell that to him. He wants to see you in his office at 10 sharp."

"What does he want to see me about?" Max asked.

"He'll tell you that," said the fireman, sliding back out of the booth. "But I would be there on time, if I was you. He's picky about that."

The fireman walked out of the diner without looking back. Max checked his watch and returned to his newspaper. The waitress came over, refilled his coffee cup, and placed a check for twenty-five cents on the table. He read the paper until ten minutes to ten, left a dollar on the table, stood, tipping his hat in the direction of the waitress now back behind the counter, and left the diner headed for the firehouse.

At ten sharp, Max stood knocking on the heavy oak door to the chief's office on the upper floor of the firehouse. The rest of the second story was one big room with metal lockers along the walls and half-a-dozen cots in two rows filling the center. He waited while the four firemen who were awake among the six lying on the cots pointedly ignored him. After a few minutes, the door opened from inside and a fireman came out, waved Max into the room, and closed the door behind him, leaving him and the chief alone in the comfortably furnished office.

The chief stayed seated in a big leather swivel chair behind an oversized desk, clear except for a leather-covered humidor. "Sit down, Ginsberg," said the chief, pointing to an armless wooden chair opposite his desk.

Max sat, holding his hat in his lap. He did not correct the chief again on his name. "You wanted to see me, Chief?" he said.

"Yeah," said the chief, "and I've got a busy morning, so let's get right down to business." Even seated, he was a full head taller than Max, and his facial expression reflected his distaste for talking to the shorter man in his well made three-piece suit.

Max asked quietly, "What kind of business is that?"

"Our partnership," said the chief.

"What partnership?"

"In your men's store," said the chief.

"I don't have any partners in my store," said Max.

"You mean the store you had, Ginsberg. It don't matter what partners you had in that store, 'cause it ain't a store anymore. What you got is a lease on a burnt-out ground-floor space that once was a store. All you got is a gutted wreck, and, I guess, a lot of bills to pay."

"That's about the size of it," said Max, "right now, at least."

"Let me ask you something, Ginsberg," said the chief. "I know you're only in this country about four years, right?"

"That's right."

"So how come you don't talk like all the other greenhorns, with their stinkin' accents from the old country?"

"I'm an American. I want to sound like an American," said Max. "So I study hard. I started on the boat coming over, and I keep it up. I have educated men coach me so I sound like what I am, an American."

"Some American," sneered the chief. "You're not even a citizen."

"Not yet, but I will be soon."

"If I say so, you will."

"What does that have to do with you, Chief?"

"If my investigation finds that you burned down your own store, you're as good as deported after you're convicted and do your time. Forget about U.S. citizen. You're an alien and a felon. You're fucking nowhere, Ginsberg, unless I save your ass."

"Look, Chief, I'd have to be crazy to burn down my own store. I'm not crazy, and I didn't burn down my store."

"You did if I say you did, Ginsberg."

"Why would you do that, when you know I didn't?"

"Well, there's no point in my givin' you a lot of bullshit. Goldberg, I might do it because I can and because it suits me, that's why."

Max sat still for a minute, his hat still on his lap. The chief opened the humidor and withdrew a cigar. He rolled it between his left thumb and index finger, then bit off the back end. He found a wooden match in the top drawer of his desk, struck it on the sole of his boot, and slowly rolled the open end of the cigar in the flame, then put the butt end in his mouth, drawing on it until he had it evenly lit, took a deep pull, and slowly blew the smoke across the desk into Max's face.

Max stood, put his hat on, and turned to leave the room.

"You leave when I say so, Goldberg," said the chief. And then he called out through the closed, oak door, "Rooney, get a couple of the lads and come in here."

The door opened immediately and three half-dressed firemen, all trailing their suspenders, came rushing into the room.

"Take this little kike downstairs and teach him some manners, boys. Then throw him out on his sheeny ass when you're finished working him over. And be sure to break something while you're at it."

The three firemen bum-rushed Max, and he held his own for a minute, knocking out cold the first guy to reach him, and starting to work on a second who was backing up, but two more bruisers came through the door, one of them swinging a policeman's billy, and they soon had Max on the floor, trying to fend off their kicks and the billy blows until they dragged him, still trying to protect himself, out the door, and then tumbling down the steps to the street floor.

"I'll be seeing you, Sheeny, before you can walk again," the chief called out after them. "You can count on that, if you don't have to use your fingers, you little Jew bastard."

When Max regained consciousness, he was lying on the sidewalk in front of the firehouse. And every part of him hurt as he took inventory, trying to figure out what was broken, besides his nose.

After a few minutes, he began to believe almost all his other parts were badly bruised and some cut, but not broken. So he dragged himself to his feet and limped to the corner where he caught a taxi to St. Mary's Hospital to have himself checked out and stitched up.

The next morning the head nurse released him, telling him he should go home and rest, after he stopped at the police station and filed a complaint. She also advised him to stay away from whoever it was that gave him the beating because he was lucky to be alive and to keep the cotton packing in his nostrils as long as he could "to help it heal as straight as possible." Max thanked the nurse, left a fifty-dollar bill as a contribution in lieu of the waived charges, and went home to bed after picking up a dozen eggs at the grocery store on his corner.

Late that afternoon one of Marchetti's men came by with a bottle of bootleg whiskey and a ham sandwich, along with his boss's invitation to drop by when he felt better. Max thanked the gangster, had two fingers of the booze, ate the sandwich, and went back to sleep for another twelve hours. The next morning he was up and out by eight and waiting at Marchetti's place by nine.

He sat in the empty office, opposite one of the empty desks, watching the door from the street until Marchetti arrived just before nine thirty and waved him into the back room.

"Sit down, Maxey," the boss said, pointing to the chair near his desk and taking his own seat behind it.

"Thanks, Mr. Marchetti."

"You sure are one tough little Jew, Maxey. I heard they beat the shit out of you and put you in the hospital."

"I put myself in the hospital after they worked me over. I wanted to make sure they hadn't broken anything besides my nose, which they made a special target. That's why I have this cotton stuffed in it. The head nurse said it would heal straighter if I kept the cotton in, even though I sound strange."

"No other serious damage?"

"Not that the hospital found, but I hurt all over, especially my kidneys where they kept kicking me with those big boots."

"Well, you're tough and lucky, I can tell you. That chief prick finds out you got nothing else broken, he'll put the boot to those firemen himself, for sure, because he wanted you in traction today.

And when he finds out you're walking around, he is really gonna be pissed."

"You figure he'll send them over to finish the job when he finds out?"

"Maybe. Stick around here for a couple of hours, and I'll have some muscle walk you home when you go. No use making it too easy for that mean bastard."

"Thanks, Mr. Marchetti. That's great."

"Nothing's for nothing. You know that."

"Sure."

"But I'm just thinking while we're talking, maybe we get two birds with one stone. You know, do a little more than just get even."

"I'm game, Mr. Marchetti."

"That I know, Maxey, and I think you're gonna like this."

"Yes, sir."

"Did he tell you what he wants from you?"

"Straight out."

"And what's that?"

"He wants to be my partner, or he'll get me charged with arson after his 'investigation' of the fire."

"Ain't that nice? He's your partner, with no investment, or you go to the can, right?"

"I think that's what he was telling me."

"And what did you say to his proposition?"

"I didn't figure it was too smart to say anything, right there in the firehouse, in his office, with his crew around. So I just got up and started to leave. He knew that was my answer, so he called his boys in and told them to work me over. I guess that was kind of his sales talk."

Marchetti leaned back in his chair, thinking for a minute, with a little smile on his face that grew broader the longer that he thought. Then he sat forward and folded his hands together on the desktop. "Oh, I think you're gonna like this . . ."

"Whatever you say, Mr. Marchetti."

"First, you gotta know, I don't like this Swede fuck. He's beginning to think this is his territory, like he's the boss around here."

"Everybody knows you are."

"He don't. And he's been working up to telling me so for a while now. He's already got a piece of a few businesses, and he takes his share in cash, no paperwork; don't give a fuck if I know it or not. No other mob guy would even dream of trying to muscle in here, but he thinks he's different, with this fire chief shit, and I won't go against him."

"That's not too smart."

"He'll learn something. But by the time he does it'll be too late."

"That sounds real good."

"Oh, you're gonna love it, Maxey. Best thing is you're gonna be ringside all the way, but you ain't ever gonna be able to tell nobody about it because you'll be doing some of the work."

"You just tell me what I do."

"Go home and take it easy today. I'll tell Gino to walk you home and get some sandwiches for you so you don't have to go out again until we pick you up this evening."

"Whatever you say, Mr. Marchetti."

"Go on now."

They walked out into the open office, and Marchetti called one of his boys over.

"You know Max, here, right?" Marchetti said.

"Sure," said Gino. "I seen him around."

"Well, you're his bodyguard today. He's had a bad night, as you can see looking at him. And I want to be sure he doesn't have any more troubles today. So you walk him home, pick up some sandwiches on the way, and see he takes a good nap. Anybody makes a move on him on the way, you take care of it. Got that?"

"Sure, Mr. Marchetti. Don't worry."

"Right. You're gonna do the worrying for me. Comes seven o'clock this evening, I'll be down on the street in front of Max's building in the big car with a couple of the other boys. As soon as you see me downstairs, you bring him down to the car, rested, ready to go. Got that?"

"Absolutely, Boss. I got it."

Marchetti turned them both toward the door to the street, patted their backs, and said, "OK, now. Get lost."

And they hustled out into the street. It was still not ten in the morning. Gino walked Max back to his apartment, dropped him off, and locked him in. Then he crossed over to the German delicatessen, picked up some sandwiches, and returned to the apartment to settle down for the day, all as instructed.

A few minutes before seven, with the street now dark, Gino took up his station looking down through the window to the sidewalk below, and almost immediately called back over his shoulder to Max, "That's the boss. Let's go," but before they closed the apartment door behind them, he asked Max if he had a muffler, and when Max said he did, told him to get it and wear it.

There were six of them in the delivery van, two of them next to the driver, in the front, holding a rolled-up rug, folded in half across their laps, and Marchetti explained the mission tersely. "The Swede always stops for a couple of pops at Bailey's on his way home. He leaves his car around the corner. So we wait at the curb near the car. When he comes to get in, Maxey walks over, pulls his muffler up around his face, comes right up behind him and says, 'Chief!' That's all, just 'Chief.' Maybe the Swede knows who it is, maybe he doesn't. Makes no difference. He'll turn around anyway; maybe start to take a swipe at Max. Soon as he turns around to Max, you two bums," he said to the front-seat boys, "run right out and bang him with the rug in the back of his knees, and make goddamn sure he stumbles before he gets his hands on Max. Soon as he loses his balance, you push him down, slap a big piece of tape over his mouth, and roll him into the rug. Gino's there to help if he's needed. But no shootin', no matter what.

"Then you pick the big bastard up and dump him in the back of the van, and we pile back in and hit the gas. Anybody fucks up's got me to deal with. Understood?"

A little after eight, the chief leaned over to insert his key into the driver's-side door of his car, and Max, the muffler covering all but his eyes, put the play in motion. Three minutes later, the rug-wrapped chief was on the floor of the van rolling east on Washington to the grate protecting the storefront of Gilman's Fabric Emporium, six blocks down the street from Max's burned-out wreck of a menswear store. Just as the van pulled up in front of Gilman's, one small, nimble specialist scampered up the west end of the grate and disconnected the burglar alarm from its power source, then jumped down to help his partner pull back the apparatus he'd just unlocked with one passkey and open the front door of the store with another.

As they opened the store door, three members of the van crew hauled the two hundred seventy-pound chief out of the van, Max following them to the sidewalk with an empty wheelbarrow they piled him into, and in less than a minute from the van's arrival, the crew and the chief were inside the darkened store. The driver had closed the door behind them, hauled the grate back into place, jumped behind the wheel, and whipped the van around the corner into a garage two blocks away.

Once inside, the crew wheeled the chief to the foot of a narrow stairway leading up to the center of a mezzanine section, beginning two-thirds of the way down the length of the store, filled with bolts of upholstery fabric in straight rows, with narrow aisles between them, stretching nearly to the back wall of the building. There was a three-foot balustrade, evenly divided on each side of the stairway, positioned at the front edge of the mezzanine to keep the bolts from tumbling down to the ground floor when they were occasionally bumped over by restocking carts maneuvering through the lanes to the cutting tables during store hours.

The chief, still wrapped head to toe in the rug, was lifted by three of the crewmen so that his upside-down figure rested on the top of the low balustrade, placing the crown of his head five-and-a-half feet above the highly polished parquet of the street-level sales floor, his feet looming another six-and-a-half feet above. On Marchetti's precise instructions, the two big men holding the chief inversely erect moved him just far enough toward the front of the store so nothing could interfere with his free fall, and then he motioned for Max to put his arms around the rug, between the other two holders, and, on the boss's count of "Three," pull him just another two inches higher and let go, just briefly hanging onto his feet as he toppled to make sure he fell headfirst. As Max felt it, from his midposition, he felt himself doing the bulk of the lifting and even more of the letting go.

The smack of the chief's huge mass cracking headfirst onto the parquet floor mimicked the muzzle blast of a howitzer, and for what seemed more than a second, he remained erect, balanced on his head, as the sound reverberated through the large room, then slowly, still nearly unbending, the immense column fell, all in one piece, to the floor, with another great, though more muffled, bang.

Marchetti, with palpable pride, said to Max, "That was some great sound, wasn't it? That's the sound of getting even. Like it?"

"The best I ever heard, Mr. Marchetti," said Max. "Absolutely the best."

The crew laughed softly, the merriment inaudible outside the store. Marchetti, smile gone, snapped to attention. "Come on now, we got ten minutes to finish the rest of the job and get out of here." He opened a carryall, and then began passing out quart bottles of kerosene, which the crew got busy spilling on the dress fabric bolts they could easily reach. When they'd spread the kerosene throughout the store and left a trail of it down the center and up onto the mezzanine, Marchetti told two of the crewmen to unroll the chief's body from the rug, reroll and , fold it, then take it to the front door he opened just a crack.

Before he instructed the crew to strike kitchen matches on the soles of their shoes and light the trail of kerosene, he had Gino check on the chief's condition.

"Not breathing," Gino reported. "I think his neck is broke."

"Light up," said Marchetti, "then get the hell out of here, and everybody wait around the corner for the van except for the close-up guys."

They lit the kerosene, starting on the mezzanine and running through the store starting blazes wherever they dropped a lighted match, then raced out the door and around the corner. The close-up team locked the front door and yanked the grate back into place, the last man scrambling up to fasten it, then following the rest of the crew around the corner where the van drove up and they piled in.

They pulled away from the curb before the team saw the first smoke curling up out of the building and were a mile away from the fire scene in less than two minutes.

Marchetti, now sitting up front with the driver, turned around to the crew and said, "Nice work, boys," all magnanimity. Then he leaned over to Max and asked, "Now, you tell me what happens from here, Maxey."

"We stop at a phone booth on the street and call in the fire, I hope."

"Smart boy," said Marchetti and patted him on the shoulder. Then, to the wheelman, "Pull over when you see a phone booth."

"Got it, Boss."

Marchetti turned back to Max. "What's the hurry to put the fire out, since we went to a lot of trouble to start it?"

"We don't want anybody living upstairs or in the buildings alongside to get burned or killed, God forbid," said Max.

"Right, again, Maxey," Marchetti said. "And we want to be sure there's plenty of the chief left to identify when his guys and the cops get to the store."

"Right," said Max.

"And . . ." Marchetti said, with a gesture of dusting off his hands, "now that they have the chief nailed at the scene, there's no more need to look around for the arsonist. Even those clowns will figure out he was the one setting the fires himself, right along."

"But, why . . ." Max started to ask, then checked himself. "I see. He pulls the same thing on every victim he pulled on me."

"Pretty good racket, eh, sonny boy? Only a guy could make a lot of enemies pullin' that kind of scam, couldn't he?"

"And some of those enemies might have the right friends, right?" said Max.

"Yeah," said Marchetti, now to the full crew. "Those things happen when you get too pushy in the wrong neighborhood. So let that be a lesson to all you guys. Never forget who the real boss is."

*   *   *

A month later, Marchetti invited Max to lunch at Giuliani's on the North Side where they were given a quiet table in the corner at the back wall, listened to the specials respectfully recited by the waiter, and ordered a modest, well prepared, antipasto misto and lasagna lunch, with a bottle of Amarone and some fresh fruit, keeping the conversation minimal until the waiter had served their espresso, the busboy cleared the table, and both attendants left them surrounded by a ring of empty tables despite the ample number of regulars occupying all the rest and a few still waiting at the bar.

"I had a long talk about you with Big Frank the other day," Marchetti opened the business discussion. "He says the top guys liked the way you handled the arson investigation, like you handle everything else that comes your way. And they have big plans for you."

"That's great," said Max. "I really appreciate it." He made a little nodding bow with his head.

Marchetti held up his right hand to stop Max from going further. "And here's where it really gets interesting, so listen close. They want you absolutely clean until further notice, no matter how long that takes. And you'll get your insurance claim paid next week so you don't have trouble with your creditors . . ."

"But I didn't—" Max began.

"You did. It's all in order, and you get the check for full reimbursement on Tuesday."

"I don't know what to say."

"Nothing is best," said Marchetti. "And you got a line of credit at Mellon Bank main branch in Pittsburgh. You just get there Wednesday when the bank opens, and you see Charles Worthy, the senior vice president, who signs up all the papers with you and opens your account, with a 50 G advance."

Max shaped his lips into a silent whistle.

"You pay off all the creditors you can remember with the insurance money, except the landlord, because he's also getting taken care of with his own insurance money. And if you forgot some creditor who turns up later with a legit claim, you pay him, too, 100 cents on the dollar, from the insurance, and you keep the 50 Gs in the bank account, less whatever you spend in walking-around money until you got things going again."

"In the old store?" Max asked.

"No. That'd take too long. Find another location."

"In Cicero?"

"For the next one, yeah. After that, wherever you want. You'll do plenty of business, wherever, because we got friends all over, and they spend money on good clothes. You just run the businesses tight and stay out of trouble. You need money for more stores and merchandise, you call Worthy, tell him what you need. You got any other kind of problem, like with wiseguys or something, you don't handle it yourself. You call me, and you leave it to me. Is that clear?

"You're strictly legit, and we're disappearing your record in New York. The little thing you had there is already gone, and the tough-guy judge just retired on his pension."

"Who owns these new stores?"

"You do. So make sure you pick good locations and run the business right. Like you know how to do."

"Mr. Marchetti, you're not kidding me?"

"No. We want a smart, clean Jew boy who knows how to make money legit. And if we ever need you to do something for us, we know where to find you, but it's never going to be for anything dirty. We got plenty of mugs for that. And they'll be some of your best customers," Marchetti laughed.

"And when do I pay back the money I borrow?"

"They're business loans to the Company you set up, and you pay them back as soon as you can, from the business profits. You get yourself a smart, legit, Jew business lawyer, and he sets up your corporations for you, all on the up-and-up. You're the only stockholder. Even if the bank gives you longer payback terms, you repay the loans and interest as fast as you can afford to, then you borrow more to keep expanding. Always the best store in the neighborhood, the best store in town, if possible. That's your business. You run it; you own it. Clear?"

"Like crystal," said Max. "And I'm not trying to be cute, but, one more time, what's your piece of this?"

"Maybe nothing. Maybe a clean, rich friend in the right place at the right time."

"But I'm nobody."

"Not for long. That's our bet."

MAX '29-'34

MAX SPENT MOST OF THE TWO DECADES FOLLOWING THE END OF The War to End All Wars building the most prestigious group of men's retail clothiers in North America and Canada under the "Landers for Men" trade style, to which he ultimately adapted his own surname. Some of his best customers were known and others suspected to be engaged in questionable pursuits, but they were unquestionably the best-dressed figures in the underworld, gradually weaned away under the discreet tutelage of his "dressy" sales personnel and old-world tailors, from their bold-patterned, broad-shouldered, handgun-accommodating broad stripes and "sharp" plaids to the Savile Row understatement of the most meticulous clubmen.

Max not only dressed himself and his clients in the toniest bespoke styles to the last detail, but under continuing private instruction by a succession of elegantly articulate, newly ordained rabbis, developed that diction, elocution, and accent which had begun to elevate the quality of sermons issuing from Reformed pulpits throughout the land. He sounded vaguely British, unmistakably refined, just barely more than audible, never vulgar or profane. And wherever he appeared, he seemed so completely comfortable that no question of his origins ever arose, virtually forgotten as they were even by those of his early benefactors who had managed to stay alive.

As the Roaring Twenties faded into the grim thirties, Max Landers extended his business interests, once quite unprofitably, into the stock brokerage business, then more and more frequently, and successfully, into oil and gas production in Oklahoma, Kansas, Texas, and Louisiana. Max had begun his forays into the "bidness" by buying relatively small participations in wells being drilled by successful oilmen he now clothed in Dallas, Houston, Tulsa, and New Orleans. By the early thirties, oil and gas prices at the wellhead had fallen so low that only the most prolific fields were still profitable. But some of Max's clients and friends were bringing in discovery wells and developing new fields which met that stringent test, and Max's sound judgment of men led him to invest in some of those winning ventures, in fact, more often than not.

Thus, while even many of the country's formerly rich were finding themselves facing hard times, Max continued to build his fortune, with "black gold" providing an ever larger share of his wealth. And when Al Capone was convicted of tax evasion and sent to Alcatraz, Max had the timely idea of explaining to some of his early wiseguy patrons how they might protect themselves from the confiscatory tendencies of the Internal Revenue Service without running afoul of the regulations that snared "Big Al."

Marchetti, still only in his late forties, had risen steadily in the hierarchy of crime in Illinois and, after Repeal, had refashioned himself as a consigliere to the Torreo family, a strategist and lobbyist whose judgment and negotiating ability had long since eclipsed his value as a muscle manager. Now he was frequently asked to arbitrate disputes in rival "families" throughout the Northern Midwest and had the prestige in his "industry" that degree of trust in his judgment implied.

He had once, in 1934, come to see Max in Dallas where they met at Max's invitation in the main dining room of the Petroleum Club. After an exchange of hugs, they discussed a $3 million deposit by Max in the First National Bank of Indianapolis, a once substantial institution which had briefly closed its doors when FDR declared the Bank Holiday in '33 and never fully recovered after its reopening.

Marchetti told Max the principal stockholders were "good people" and had earned a lot of respect with their stand-up behavior after Repeal when the bootlegging profits had to be replaced by expansion in unions, prostitution, gambling, and pornography, and, in some cases, narcotics, where not every family had established footholds or wanted them. The Indianapolis bank had to fund what were essentially new businesses for operators who had learned their trades in a more accommodating environment under the Volstead Act.

"Who's the payee I write on the check?" Max asked.

"You don't have it in green?"

"Don't worry, Mr. Marchetti. My check is good."

"But these guys are used to dealing in cash, Max."

"Believe me, the bank will be happy to take my check and like it better that way. They'll advance the funds, wherever they have to go, the day they get my check."

"You don't need time to pull it together?"

"I've been waiting for this call ever since Repeal, Mr. Marchetti. You and your friends made me, then you left me completely alone to build what I've built absolutely legally. Now some of those friends need my help. That's all I need to know. They've got it. And if they ever need more, and you give me a little time, they can have that, too. Whatever I've got."

Marchetti shook his head. "I didn't even hear that. And nobody's gonna hear it from me. The idea always was for you to get rich legit and stay that way," he said. "If we ever do need some help sometime, we're not bashful. We'll ask for it. Odds are, we don't ever have to ask for it again."

"Just so you know, it's always going to be there if you or your friends need it. And I'll start putting some cash away in a few safe-deposit boxes so we don't have to keep leaving paper trails in the future."

"Good boy, Max, but you're sure you can really do this now?"

Max drew a folding pad of checks out of his inside breast pocket, filled in a portion of the first one, and looked across the table at Marchetti. "I still need to know who's the payee."

"Just First National Bank of Indianapolis," said Marchetti.

Max entered the details on the stub, filled out and signed the check, folded and handed it to Marchetti, who glanced at it, nodded with his lips pursed, and put it in the outside breast pocket of his suit coat. Then he looked directly into Max's eyes. "That's a lot of walking-around money, Max," he said with no special emphasis.

Max answered quietly, "Thanks to you and your friends, I've done all right."

Marchetti said, "I don't know when you get it back."

"I'll get it when they have it to give me. That's fine with me."

Marchetti half stood up at his chair, leaned over, and offered his right hand to shake with Max, then reached up with his left to ruffle the neatly trimmed hair on the back of Max's head.

"You're all right, Maxey. You done real good, like I knew you would. You take care now." Then he began to pull himself back to turn and leave, but Max held onto his right hand.

"Mr. Marchetti," Max said softly, nearly at a whisper, "there may be something you could do for me that could turn out very well for you, too."

Marchetti sat back down. "You got a problem, Max?"

"No," Max said. "But I think some of your good friends might, and I could help."

"With Repeal, the Depression, and every ambitious prosecutor in the country trying to take down his own Al Capone, my friends got plenty of problems. But you just did your share." He touched the pocket where he had placed the check. "So now go back to your own business, and stay out of trouble, including our trouble. You hear me? My friends are big boys. Let them handle their own headaches. They give enough of them."

"Will you hear me out, Mr. Marchetti?"

"Yeah, I'll hear you out. But we're going to make a change, right now, first. You just graduated, Maxey. From now on I'm Carlo to you."

"No, Mr. Marchetti. That wouldn't feel right to me."

"But you'll get used to it. No bullshit, now. That's it. From now on, I'm Carlo to you, with anybody. Got it?"

"If you're going to insist."

"I just did. That's it. And I got a new name for you, too."

"What's that? My new name."

"Duke."

"Duke? Come on."

"It's what you sound like. Not just a gent. You sound like a fucking duke. And the way your nose healed with just a little bump, looks like you got it playing some high-class sport. God knows you dress like one. That's the way you handle yourself, too. So that's what I'm gonna call you: The Duke. But mostly just Duke. Get used to it. And, at least for a while, anybody calls you Duke, you'll know I sent 'em. Then pretty soon everybody'll call you Duke, and they won't all be from me anymore. But remember, first I made you somebody, then I made you rich, and now I'm making you The Duke."

"I really have to laugh, Mr . . . ."

Marchetti raised his hand, palm out, like a traffic cop.

"I mean, Carlo. That's going to take some getting used to."

"Live with it. Now, what's on your mind, Duke?"

"Aren't any of your, friends, I mean the big guys, worrying about what happened to Capone?"

"Like, are they sorry for him, poor Big Al, all jammed up in the joint? Don't ever let anybody knows Capone hear you say that. He tells Big Al and Capone'll put out a contract on you. He's not the kind of guy who wants sympathy. That's not for him. He's a mean prick, but he's no crybaby. Hears you say so, and you're good as dead."

"All right. Then we'll have to find some other way to say this, but your friends have to know, particularly the biggest ones, that they can all end up where Capone is," Max said.

"You think they don't know that? The shit they're into, they know these crazy prosecutors all want to be governor or president, if they can turn two rats and seat a jury, Mr. Big is in the Big House with Alphonse."

"But they don't have to, that's my point."

"They all gonna get amnesty, or something?"

"I'm not suggesting that."

"Then what the hell are you saying?" Marchetti grumbled, a little exasperated.

"I'm saying I can show them how to avoid going to jail on tax evasion charges, like Capone."

"Sure," Marchetti came back. "All they have to do is pay taxes. They're really gonna do that. They're gonna march right into the IRS office and give 'em a big check, like all good citizens, right?

"Are you fucking nuts? Or maybe they just bring in a suitcase full of cash. How's that? They're always trying to figure out how to launder green. So that works great. They bring the cash right to the feds. No problem. Pick it up next Saturday, just like shirts from the Chink's. Clean as a whistle."

"No, Carlo. A lot better than that."

"I'm listening, Duke."

"The first thing is that they do have to file tax returns and declare a certain amount of gross income, from all sources, each year."

"And where they got it from?"

"Yes."

Marchetti smiled. Then he said, "Sure. I can see, say Joe Adonis, counting it all up and writing it down on a tax form. Gambling: 500 Gs. Prostitution: 500 Gs. Loan Sharking: 700 Gs. Protection: 300 Gs. Found on the street: 200 Gs. I make that 2 million 2, in round numbers. What do I owe you?"

Max laughed. "Not exactly like that, Carlo. First, Joe takes all of that green and puts it into the businesses of smart regular people he knows who are making good money in their businesses. Then those guys who own the businesses put him on their payrolls, or whatever else they do when they're laundering money for him now, so he gets out a weekly check that gives him back almost all the cash he puts into the business. Maybe a little more, if Joey is also providing protection, or fixing the guys up with showgirls, or whatever. That's the money he declares to the government on his tax return. The laundered money."

"OK," Marchetti said, "so he's washed his money. What's the big deal?"

"I'm just getting to the good part, Carlo. Let me go on."

"I ain't got all day, Duke, even for you," Marchetti said, looking at his watch. "I got an appointment with the barber in twenty minutes."

"Now, Carlo," Max went on, "Joey or his accountant or his lawyer, whoever looks after his money, takes that nice clean money he was just paid in commissions and expenses and bonuses and invests it in the same thing H. L. Hunt, and J. P. Getty and half the richest people in this country invest their money in these days. Drilling oil wells."

"What so great about that?" Carlo asked.

"In the first place," Max explained, "almost all the money invested in drilling oil wells is a legitimate deductible business expense in the year it's invested, and that deduction cancels out the tax liability on the investor's other income. So instead of paying out the money to the feds in taxes, the investor pays it to an oil and gas production company for a share in the wells it's drilling."

"What if the wells don't hit oil?" Carlo asked.

"Sometimes they don't, so the investor loses his investment and might just as well have paid the taxes in the first place."

"So, not so great, right?"

"Right," Max said. "But if, say Joe, is investing with the right people, most of the time he's going to get enough oil to pay back everything he's invested, sometimes ten, twenty, a hundred times over. And, here's the really interesting part: there's something called the depletion allowance which makes almost half the payback he gets tax free."

"This is legal?" Carlo asked, skeptical.

"The oil part, what I've been explaining, absolutely, and it's what all the smart money, big smart money, in Texas and Louisiana and Oklahoma and Kansas, is doing, coining money, paying their taxes, and smiling all the way to the bank."

"What's wrong with it?" Carlo shook his head again. "Must be something. Otherwise it's a license to steal."

"Well, first, Joe has to figure out his own way to turn his illegal cash income into reportable income he can declare on a tax return. That's a problem he's always got, and I don't touch it. I don't get into that."

"What else?"

"Joe could run into very bad luck or a very bad operator. Either one could cost him money."

"You vouch for the operator?"

"Yes, but not the luck every time. He could roll cold dice once in a while, but the serious operators I know are like the house. They don't lose big or for long."

Carlo leaned in and said very quietly, "With guys like Joe, they wouldn't live long enough to have much of a bad run, and neither would you or me."

Max sat back and opened his hands palms up over the table. "Only two sure things, in life, right?"

"Death and taxes," Carlo finished.

They sat for a moment.

"What's in it for you, Duke?"

"I invest right beside Joe," Max answered.

"Retail?"

"Best price, and I see that Joey gets that, too."

"And me?"

"You want me to carry you for something, you just tell me, and you've got it."

Carlo thought for a moment. Then, "Not for openers. If it goes as good as you say, we can talk later."

"Whatever you say, whenever you say."

They sat silently again until Carlo finally said, "I'll see what I can set up that keeps you clean. I gotta get to the barber now. I'll call you at your office." Then he stood up, leaned over the table and placed his right hand gently against Max's cheek for a second, turned, and walked away. But not far. He stopped at a phone booth in the lobby and put in a call to a partner in one of the top accounting firms in Chicago.

Ten days later, Max was sitting in the CPA's office just after 11 a.m., exchanging credentials in what began as a cordial sort of interview. The accountant, John Halladay, was big, bluff, Irish, and respectful. Max noticed three of the framed certificates on the wall behind him announced that he also had a law degree and was a member of the Cook County and State of Illinois Bar Associations.

He said he had been told that "The Duke," as he called Max, was a solid guy he could talk to freely. He made a point of saying he confirmed that report very carefully, and everything had come back "aces." He apologized for not knowing Duke himself by reputation and explained he had to be particularly careful "these days," although his initial vetting results made him very comfortable skipping some of the usual checks and double checks.

Max thanked him for the "compliments" and reviewed his proposal, finding the accounting partner at least as knowledgeable as he on the tax issues and not totally unfamiliar with the oil business. Max said if there was anything Halladay wanted to know, he'd be happy to explain, but the deal was not very complicated.

The investing entities were limited partnerships with corporate entities controlled by the heavy-hitting operators' companies as general partners and Halladay's clients, what the operators called "et als," as Limited Partners with no liability whatsoever beyond their defined investments. Halladay was familiar with the format and recognized the names of the big hitters Max identified. He also understood that each one of them had his own style, but none of them wanted any input from the "et als" except their cash.

They talked about scale and Halladay said he was prepared to start with at least $5 million from five of his clients and have the money spread over three operators Duke would endorse without qualification. He explained that he would be the agent for all of his clients, acting with a power of attorney and making the investments in his own name, having clearly anticipated that the operators might not be comfortable with his clients' own names on their books.

Duke said his own lawyer would handle all the paperwork with Halladay and could start drafting immediately. Then he asked Halladay how much money, at the maximum, he could see his clients investing a year, if the "projects" performed as expected. Halladay said that the amount was potentially unlimited, conceivably running to hundreds of millions a year. Duke told him that potential would be very appealing to his operators because they were anxious to drill a greater percentage of deeper, more expensive wells, where the risks were higher, but the rewards disproportionately better, too, and spreading the risk over more wells would be sound business strategy for them no matter how good the prospects looked on paper.

Halladay's expression grew very serious, and he said, slowly and with great emphasis, "You and your people should bear in mind that my clients are notoriously sore losers."

"These Texans are the same way," said the Duke. "They have big reputations and big egos, so they play to win. But they do drill dry holes as well as producers. That goes with the territory. If you think your clients want to minimize risk and give up some upside to get it, we can allocate their investments accordingly. I don't think they'll do as well in the long run as they would with the mix the operators create for themselves. They are the best in the business, so doing what they do is the smart bet, in the long run. But you, or you and your clients, have to decide what kind of a mix you want."

"I don't have to ask them," Halladay answered. "They want it both ways. Small risk, big profits."

"Can't be guaranteed," Duke said.

"Let me talk to them and get back to you."

Duke said that was fine, and he would wait while Halladay and his clients made their decisions. A week later he got the call in his Dallas office.

"They want a mix," Halladay said. "Lowest risk they can get and highest profit they can get for taking that risk."

"OK," Duke said. "That's rational. Give me some idea of the size for the first go-round, and let me see what I can do."

"We'll actually take $10 million for openers. But remember," Halladay said, "we both have a lot at stake with this," then rang off.

Duke had his secretary place three calls and leave messages. All three were returned that morning, two by principals, one by an attorney. Three investments totaling $10 million were made for Carlo's friends before noon, and Duke added half a million to each for his own account. All the deals were on telephone handshakes, with paperwork to follow. Duke guaranteed delivery of the investors' funds at the call of the operators before the first wells were "spudded." All three operators guaranteed "industry" terms.

Before the day was over, Duke had graduated from the role of an occasional, relatively moderate-scale investor with his top-rank custom tailoring customers to a "reliable partner" with major potential. He was a player, among players, and no one knew his sources or his limits.

DANNY '89

I HAD THREE MORE MEETINGS WITH DANNY'S LAWYER BEFORE THE END of the year, each time papering up a purchase of stock or options or both on Wyco Pharmaceuticals. He was already well over 5 percent beneficial ownership and was therefore technically "a reporting party" when he bought or sold the company's common stock or equivalents. So McGuiness had an agreement with Danny's office to call him before they placed any orders in Wyco for his various accounts.

It was still possible that Danny was just building a trading position and had no designs on control. Some traders did take very big positions and still avoided running the businesses or trying to influence management, and Danny could have been one of those, or a potential greenmailer planning to make enough problems for the management to get himself bought out by the company at a profit without the trouble or the expense of a proxy fight. In any event, I didn't think I had to worry about him or his maneuvers since he wasn't my client and neither was Wyco. So long as Danny reported properly, and I believed I could count on McGuiness to see to that, Connelly could continue to represent any sellers referred to us and charge them our regular, lofty, hourly rates for work that was neither original nor burdensome, except for a bit of extra time pressure.

Early in the New Year, McGuiness asked me to lunch with him at the Knick, and with the "no papers" rule in effect in the dining room, we kept the conversation light until we had each ordered our Martinis and grilled soles and the waiter had left our corner table.

Then McGuiness, in his dry, soft-spoken manner, immediately broached his subject. "It will come as no surprise to you, I'm sure, Peter, that my client has decided he wants to run a slate of his own."

"No, Martin, despite his representations to the contrary, I am not at all surprised. But have you looked over his public statements and his filings to be sure he hasn't boxed himself in?"

"I have." McGuiness smiled, the soul of propriety.

"Just to avoid any question of his having been misleading, in any way?"

"Of course," said McGuiness. "That's our standard practice . . ."

"When your client does a 180."

"In all cases."

"Starting with his original purchase," I said, "and right up to date."

"All in order. Just a change of mind."

"Is he going to bother making an explanation?" I asked, without inflection.

"Not if he doesn't have to. It's uncertain territory, to be avoided, preferably."

"We'll see how far that plan goes, won't we, if we go to trial?"

McGuiness leaned over to speak very softly to me. "Now why would that ever happen, Peter?"

"I could see it coming up if someone really wanted to push the point."

"Peter," McGuiness said, "let's not borrow any trouble. Miller hasn't done anything wrong and doesn't plan to, on my watch. So cut him a little slack. He's entitled to change his mind."

"If he knew what his game plan was all along, he didn't change his mind. He intentionally misled the company and the shareholders. That's a violation."

"Only Miller knows that."

"Maybe so, maybe not."

"What's that supposed to mean?"

"Maybe his lawyer always knew what was really on his mind."

"I resent that implication, Peter. It's way out of line."

"But whatever he told you is privileged, isn't it? So we'll never know, will we?"

"You're a big rule man, Peter. And we both know that one." He sat back in his chair, crumpling his linen napkin in his right hand. "I made this date with you as a courtesy, Cowen, but you're not exactly returning it in kind."

"Then let me take this discourtesy a little further while I'm at it, Mr. McGuiness. If Danny was really just planning on making a passive investment, why did he need a top securities lawyer to advise him on it? In the unlikely event that your client hasn't told you, I have some history with him, and it's not good. With more than adequate reason, I don't trust him. And I also don't appreciate being set up by him and his lawyer." I folded my own napkin and placed it on the tablecloth. "So, if you'll excuse me, I'm leaving." I stood at the side of the table, said, "Thanks for the courtesy," and walked away.

McGuiness, in a voice a bit louder than was acceptable in that decorous dining room, called after me, "Don't mention it, Counselor, but consider yourself on notice. The battle is joined."

I picked up my Burberry downstairs on the way out and walked down Fifth to my office at 30 Rockefeller Plaza. Then I crossed over to the skating rink for a bit more air and gradually cooled off before heading upstairs to my desk. I sat with my face to the window, looking down over the flags flaring in the wind below and thought through my position.

After about ten minutes, I decided the situation was not as dire as in my anger I had felt it to be. I had been snookered, of course, and would have to advise Arthur of how the gambit had developed. But everyone knew Danny played at the edges of sanctionable behavior, and McGuiness had the reputation of deserving his client. I had been embarrassed and arguably overreacted, but I'd lost nothing except a bit of face I could win back if my path and McGuiness's ever crossed again, as was very likely.

I had just met the woman I would soon marry, Audrey Harman, and we had begun seeing each other exclusively. She was an actress and aspiring theatre director who had grown up in the northern suburbs of Chicago, done her undergraduate and drama school work at Northwestern, and just began an off-Broadway stint in a new comedy the producers were trying to move to Broadway. For a while, we were totally absorbed in her theatre world, spending our limited leisure time with her friends and essentially dropping out of the ultramoneyed Upper East Side, Hamptons, and Fairfield County set in which I had occasionally run into Danny. And after the McGuiness clash, he didn't push any business my way at Connelly for a while.

But Danny's net seemed to pull in everyone we both knew from secondary school and Yale, along with all the newer acolytes his money and glamour attracted, so it was almost impossible to avoid at least indirect contact between us, socially or at the office. One member of our Horace Mann tennis team (then Monroe Goldberg, now Matt Golden) was doing well in his own right on Wall Street as a dealer in and very "visible" authority on options trading. He had published a popular book on the subject, experted it on television occasionally, and was a major earner at his own firm. He was not in Danny's league as a "master of the universe," but was a well publicized success who brought his personal business to me at Connelly, both "for old times' sake" and because, as he said, he had always respected me. He had never been quite inner-circle with Danny and me and assumed we were still as close as ever.

"Well, you know Danny," Golden said, holding his coffee cup and saucer on his knee, master's tea style, as we sat in facing chairs in my office. "He can just bury you with business. The guy is absolutely amazing, and he must send me twenty accounts a week with this new deal of his."

"What's that?" I asked, still on the hook, to my own irritation.

"That takeover he's planning. You've got to know all about it."

"Not really," I said.

"The Wyco thing, you know. Oh, I forgot, you can't discuss another client's business with me. I understand. Forget it."

"No," I said. "I don't represent Danny."

"So you really don't know about the deal?"

"That's right, I don't want to. And unless what you want to discuss relates directly to your personal interests, I don't want to know anything about any deal I can't read in the newspaper."

"Well," Golden said, "it's a little complicated."

"Let's try to keep it simple," I told him. "I really don't want to know anything about Danny's business that isn't already public information."

"But I'm here to get your advice."

I asked him if the advice he wanted had anything to do with Danny.

"In a way, yes."

I thought for a minute, then I told him, "Matt, I believe you ought to get your advice on this matter from somebody else. I'm happy to have you as a client, but Danny and I have a history that makes it, let's say, a little sticky for me to represent you in something involving him. I'm sorry. On anything else, I'm very pleased to be your lawyer, and I hope you'll give me that opportunity. But I'm going to pass this one."

"Man, Peter, you sure have a strange way of practicing law."

"It's a strange situation."

"Peter, you don't even know what I want to talk about. Why don't you hear me out, and then decide if you want to advise me. I'm an old friend who is asking you for legal counsel and ready, willing, and able to pay top rates for it. Doesn't that qualify for a hearing in your book?"

"I wish it did, Matt, but—"

"Then hear me out, damn it!" Golden smacked the arm of his chair.

"OK, Mon . . . , I mean Matt," I said, shaking my head. "I think I'm going to regret this, but let's hear it." And I walked around to sit behind my desk, facing him.

Then I heard just what I didn't want to hear. Danny was urging all of his substantial network of friends and contacts to buy as much Wyco Pharmaceutical as they could afford, and, also on Danny's advice, most of them were buying "out of the money" puts on the common from Matt Golden's firm, increasing their costs but protecting their downside.

Matt kept increasing the strike price, sometimes several times a day, but he had already run out of capital to keep covering his position by going long more of the stock, and Danny kept adding to the pressure with more buying, both in the stock and the puts. The shorts had already covered once and some of them were taking new positions, if they could borrow the stock, but that only increased demand and moved the trading price and the put strike price higher still.

Danny had not announced his intention to make a bid for the company or whispered it to his intimates. But the market was delivering the news, as the stock kept making new highs, and Matt's exposure on the puts reached rapidly increasing multiples of his capital. Matt had gone to see Danny at his office, both to thank him for the business and to tell him he couldn't handle any more. Danny asked him how much more money he needed. Matt knew the number to the penny as of close of business the previous day because his controller was pounding the table over it and threatening to quit before the NASD caught up with them and shut them down.

"I need three million two just to get in ratio with what I have out," Matt said, "and every piece of new business I book gins that up higher."

Danny asked him to calm down and told Matt he would have the money wired to his account at Marine Midland from overseas the next day, plus another million for breathing room. And he told him to forget about being blown out, because Danny would cover any losses he might have writing the puts.

Matt told Danny he wasn't losing money; in fact, he was making big profits on paper, just hemorrhaging cash, but no longer worried if Danny was guaranteeing any losses and covering his capital shortfall. Danny sent him away happy and committed to selling the puts as long as Danny made him whole.

But Matt explained to me that he wasn't a gambler, was "really" very risk averse, compulsive about being in control of his business, and, while he had great faith in Danny, didn't like being dependent upon anyone else for the survival of his company.

Then the discussion went on something like this:

"Why don't you close the positions and pack it in?"

"Because I don't have the cash to do that, without Danny's help."

"How about matching calls?" I pushed the point.

"That sounds good, but it still gives me too big a book for my capital."

"Then tell Danny you want out."

"I've as much as said that, but Danny says I'm a big boy and I knew what I was getting into, which is partly true."

"If he's doing what I think he's doing," I said, "you've got plenty of leverage."

"Meaning?" Matt asked.

The current proxy solicitation rules, as I've said, had not yet evolved. So I had to think and speak very carefully.

"He's probably got deals going that put him way over the threshold. So he should be reporting the trades he guarantees through you, as well as his own trades," I finally said.

"How would you know if he was or wasn't?"

"If he's filing, I'd see it. If he's not, I'd see that, too," I told him.

"And?"

"I don't think I can tell you."

"What the hell does that mean, Peter? Don't I have a right to know?"

"Not from me, necessarily," I said. "Why don't you ask Danny? You're certainly entitled to know from him."

"What if he doesn't tell me the truth?"

"Just ask him, and see what he says."

"How do I know if it's true, whatever he says?"

"You have to make that judgment yourself."

"But I'm asking you to be my lawyer and tell me what to do," Matt nearly whined.

"I can't be your lawyer in this matter," I said, "much as I'd like to help you. I'm conflicted out."

"You mean, you're representing Danny?"

"No, I'm not."

"Then what's the conflict?"

"It's a close call, but I believe I have a conflict. That's all I can tell you."

"That's just great, Peter, my old friend. I come to you in trouble, and it's too close a call for you to help me. That's just fucking great."

"I'm sorry, Matt. I think you should get another lawyer."

"Fucking great, Peter. Thanks a million. Make that twenty million, which is about what I'm now on for."

"I'm sorry, Matt. And this is not legal advice, but why don't you figure out a pattern of calls you can buy that will net out your position, or set up some collars, whatever works, to cancel most of your risk without having to bank on Danny? Doesn't that make sense?"

"Locking in losses? Stick to the law, Peter. You obviously don't know shit about option trading." Matt stood up, shaking his head, and walked out of the room. With the doorknob in his hand, he turned back and said, "You're not out of this yet, Peter," and slammed the door behind him.

MAX '31

Max felt he could run the retail business from any city where he had a store, and with his increasing involvement in the oil business, he decided to move his main office to Dallas, where he had two. He leased space in a new downtown office tower and bought a just completed home in one of the baronial developments on the West side. He then began asking some of his more established local clients for recommendations on interior designers. Barney Graham, a third-generation oilman in his mid-fifties who had impressed him with his style in dress and manner, took the inquiry seriously and explained that he had a recommendation he would make with confidence, if Max could get the designer to work for him.

Max asked why that should be a problem, and Graham explained that although she happened to be his daughter, who had come back to Dallas three years before, after studying at Parsons and putting in several years as an assistant to Dorothy Draper, she was the most sought after designer in Texas. In that brief period, despite rock-bottom oil prices, she had become a stunning success, according to Graham, with a waiting list of wealthy clients and multiple projects in work all the time. Barney said he would put in a word for Max but couldn't guarantee anything because Betsy Graham made "all her own decisions, on everything."

Max got her telephone number from Graham's secretary and called her three times from his hotel suite, leaving messages with her office each time, getting no calls back, before she happened to pick up the phone herself when he called, one last time, on the odd chance he might catch her at 7 p.m.

"You're a very persistent man, Mr. Landers," she said. "Now tell me what's so important."

"I understand that you're the best interior designer in the city, and I'd like you to design my new home and my new offices," Max told her, figuring he shouldn't risk her brushing him off if he dawdled.

"My dad says you're a self-made man and a gentleman that he really likes, so I'd love to help you, especially because that self-made part isn't as common as it used to be in Dallas, although the gentleman part is getting to be a little more so. But, really, I just have more work than my associates and I can handle at the moment. Let me make a referral for you."

"Only if you make that recommendation over lunch or a drink."

"Why not breakfast at the Dillon tomorrow at eight?"

"Done," said Max. "I'll be waiting for you."

And he was, sitting at a table overlooking the formal garden when she walked in stride for stride with the maître d'hôtel, straight to his table. He stood to shake her hand, and she shook his like a tennis pro gripping a racquet. She was an inch taller than he and smiling with her mouth and eyes, her sandy blond hair cut short and curly, wearing just light lipstick, in brown slacks and a tan tweed sport jacket over a white blouse open at the neck. In Duke's not uninformed opinion, dazzlingly beautiful.

"Hi, Daddy's buddy," she said.

"Max Landers, and I'm delighted to meet you," he said.

"Duke to your friends, Barney tells me," she said, sitting opposite him as the maître d'hôtel pulled out her chair.

"He's a lovely man, a terrific friend, and a great oil finder."

"He's all that. And a good father, if a little too doting. He was a wonderful husband, too, but he lost my mother six years ago and doesn't have any interest in marrying again, much as I'd love to see him do it."

"Does he know much about interior design?"

She raised an elegant finger, and as the waiter leaned in, ordered "Juice, fruit, toast, and coffee, please, Aaron," smiling. "And you, Mr. Landers?"

He ordered the same.

Betsy resumed. "As to Barney's taste in design, it's damn good. My mother and the local doyenne did their home, years back, and it's a little overstated. But he did his own office, with the grand dame's assistant running errands and Barney making all the decisions. It's great. I mean that. I couldn't do better myself today, maybe not as well. He's just very good at anything he does, and if you make his clothes, you know he has impeccable taste. The best in town."

"That's what he says about you."

"Are you Max or Duke? He calls you both."

"It's just some sort of joke some people have picked up."

"You're really not nobility? Could have fooled me. You do sound special."

"That's because I learned the English language a little late," Duke said, "and from instructors who had a special kind of British accent I picked up."

"Intentionally," she said, as much a statement as a question.

Duke hesitated a moment before answering. Then he said, very deliberately damning the torpedoes, "I studied English and speech under a series of young men who were graduates of a seminary that trained Reformed rabbis, and they spoke the way I do now, which is, I'm told, kind of Oxbridge. I liked the way they sounded, so I learned to speak the same way."

Betsy put her fruit spoon down on the service plate and leaned in toward him, speaking softly, "Max," she asked, "are you Jewish?"

"Yes," he said. "Not very observant but certainly Jewish."

"Does my dad know that?"

"I haven't any idea."

"Guess."

"Perhaps not. I don't remember it ever coming up with us. Why do you ask?"

"Because I doubt if my father even knows many Jewish people, except maybe for the Marcuses and the Neimans, a few lawyers and a doctor or two."

"So?" said Max, a little defensive and definitely ready for anything.

Betsy looked carefully, with her designer's eye, at the elegantly dressed man across the table. She noted, particularly, the even features, deep set dark brown eyes, slightly thickened bridge of his longish, straight nose, the thin, wide lips turned up at the ends in a nascent smile, the deep lines extending outward from the edges of his nostrils to the ends of his lips, and the strong chin, all symmetrically arranged under a cap of closely cropped, slightly graying hair. She liked what she saw as intelligence and determination in that attractive, virile face.

"Well, Max Landers," she said, folding her hands in front of her on the edge of the table, "I've just decided I'm going to make room for your two assignments in my design practice, starting now, and for you in my personal life starting with dinner tonight, after we go visit your two places at five this afternoon, if that's all right with you. And I'd better let my dear daddy know what he's in for before it's too late."

"Too late for what?"

"Not to say anything he'd be sorry for," she said, leaving no doubt about the kind of thing she meant.

"You are a very decisive person, Betsy."

"That's definitely true, Duke," she said.

Betsy always made it her business to find out a good deal about her client's interests and habits when she took one on. Max found the exercise fascinating and productive on two levels. She designed his office and his home exactly as he liked to think he would have created them himself, if he had enough knowledge of the art and the trade. And when he asked her to marry him, after two months of relatively chaste intimacy, she felt she knew him well enough to say she would.

Barney really didn't get very worked up over the religion factor; said, in fact, that he probably would have guessed Duke at least had some Jewish blood in him, if anyone had asked, but no one had. And when he thought about it himself, in the apparent context, he concluded he had no inclination to challenge Betsy's judgment.

Besides, he and the Duke were already friends, and the thought of having a son-in-law who got along with him, adored his daughter, and could apparently afford to give her whatever she wanted, seemed more than good enough reasons to give them his blessings. He did check out Duke's A1 financial standing through his bank, and he did ask the couple in what faith they intended to bring up their children. Betsy ended that discussion by saying that she and Max would give the subject appropriate consideration when the time came.

They decided to have the wedding when the house she was designing for Duke was ready for them to move in together, and that meant at least a six-month delay, as Betsy calculated it. In deference to Barney, who never specifically made the request, they maintained separate residences in the interim, Betsy in her "statement" apartment on the top floor of the tallest residential building in town and Duke in a home he rented from a friend of Barney's, fully staffed, on the Dallas Country Club grounds, although Duke was not yet a member. The friend did arrange for Duke to have guest privileges at the club, which he chose not to use.

Those were busy times, often hectic, with both of them tending to their active businesses, planning the wedding, and finishing first Duke's office, and then their home. And they were finding they were not always in agreement on matters that came up for the first time and a few carryovers from earlier discussions, as well. But neither one had any appetite for acrimony, and what they couldn't resolve civilly, they agreed to revisit from time to time until they had found an acceptable compromise.

Betsy had seen her father go along with her mother's strong feelings, even when he didn't agree, confident that he could hold his ground when he felt it was necessary. And she believed her parents' marriage had been a good one, as long as it lasted. Max's mother had ruled the roost benevolently in Danzig, and Max seemed to have no pressing need to assert himself at home, any more than had his father, as he remembered his childhood.

But Max, in business, was another man. He and Barney had enjoyed three consistently successful years in building oil and gas reserves, Barney for Graham Energy, his vehicle, and Max for his own account and his investors'. For those years, Barney was the most productive of the big-time oil finders Max invested with, and "The Duke" took the dry holes without complaint, as costs of doing business, so long as Barney delivered solid aggregate results each year. They had no real argument until shortly before Betsy and Max married. But that contention set the tone for them thereafter; trustful but wary, ready to become adversarial with proper provocation, any time, over any amount.

Barney's geologist and land man had found and negotiated a lease on a quarter section they believed had been overlooked on the eastern edge of the Permian Basin because it lay "down dip" (in trade terminology) of a small field that had been quickly depleted in the early exploitation of the basin. The geologist believed he saw surface evidence of a fault at depth that had occurred after the Devonian sediments had been laid down thinly over the crest of an older anticline and thickened as they accumulated along the slopes of the structure, then been thrust further down by the later occurring fault. Once they had persuaded Barney of their argument, he not only funded the purchase of the original 160, but also sent the land man out to lease the balance of three full sections surrounding the depleted field.

After the parameters of the original, limited discovery had been established, the "play" moved south and west, leaving the displaced strata along the flanks of the feature untested. Barney proposed to drill all the way through the downthrown sequence, hoping that the hydrocarbons it seemed reasonable to him to believe had been trapped along the flanks of the feature before the fault occurred were still trapped where they now lay "down dip."

Max, for himself and his investors, took 49.5 percent the working interest, 24.75 percent for Max and the same for his "et als" as joint venturers with Barney, who retained 50.5 percent. In his standard deal with the operator, Max protected his investors by insisting that the operator "turnkey" the drilling, testing, and completion of the "wildcat" at a fixed price for each function, and since his commitment to his investors was that they would always pay the same price he did, Barney had to turnkey to Max, as well, pro rata. The arrangement was unusual for exploratory wells (although familiar in development wells where the unexpected costs were less of a risk), but Max now wielded a lot of money and it, as usual, tended to dictate less than critical details of terms.

The well was projected to 8,500 feet as the deepest to that date in the Eastern Permian, and the "turnkey" for a dry hole to total depth was priced at $1,600,000 without testing; a single completion in the Devonian, with testing, at $2,400,000. The well moved smoothly through the rock sequence and was, apparently, continuously in oil—and gas-bearing strata, with the cuttings proving the fault theory, until it encountered the top of the Devonian just above 7,200 feet, hit a high pressure gas cap, and knocked the blowout preventer stack off the well, sending a plume of gas soaring two hundred feet into the twilight sky, which the drilling rig operator quickly lit and turned into a blazing torch visible for fifty miles. The blowout did some damage to the rig but caused no serious injuries to personnel, and a well-killing crew from Midland was called in as quickly as it could get to the site.

For Barney, who had himself flown down from Dallas on the news, these interim results were sweet evidence supporting the theory behind the well, and he had been running the potential profit numbers in his head, at various levels of production, through the half-hour flight from Dallas Hobby, assuming the high-pressure gas was a cap on a substantial new oil field, and he was happily containing his excitement as he pitched in with his drilling staff and the contractor's men to get the emergency under control as soon as he reached the site. It wasn't until hours later that it dawned on him that the "turnkey" arrangement would cost him a lot of money, since he would be paying 100 percent of the debacle costs for his 50.5 percent interest in the new field discovery, if it was one.

Everybody on the scene and new specialists arriving by the hour worked all night to get the well under control, although the prospects of using the current hole to reach total depth did not look good. That tentative judgment, if sustained, threatened to double the cost of the discovery well (as the assembled professionals generally agreed it was likely to be) before adding in the cost of any equipment damage, beyond the BOP stack, which was insured. It was plain to anyone present that Barney Graham was cool under fire and knew his business, but as he moved about identifying problems and approving actions, calm and commanding throughout, he was working up a silent fury over the deal his immediately prospective son-in-law had "roped him into" with the "turnkey nonsense."

By the time he'd been driven back to Dallas by one of his field managers as the sun rose ahead of them, he was planning how to present the mixed news to Max and unload the turnkey harness as quickly as possible. Back at his home by 8:00 a.m., he told his houseman, Pedro, to call Max and set a breakfast meeting for the Petroleum Club just as soon as he could shower, shave, dress, and get there, for each step of which process Pedro knew the timing to the minute.

Max was waiting for him at a corner table in the dining room and had ordered juice, toast, eggs, bacon, and coffee for them, making sure to have it served piping hot, as Barney liked it, except for the juice, the minute Barney sat down.

Max stood to shake hands with Barney, and they each pulled their chairs in to the table, talking softly to avoid being overheard. "So how goes our very interesting new well?" Max asked.

"Good news and bad news, Max. I think there's a very good chance the well is a significant discovery, and we've got the whole three sections around it, paying just the landowners' eighth royalty, and no bonus because nobody liked the play. There could be at least four wells to the section. And I don't have to tell you, but I will again anyway, that over the last five years just about everybody in the business dismissed this prospect because the sands were so thin at the crest in the old well.

"My only problem is that damned turnkey drilling contract you made me give those investors of yours and you, too. Which is why I wanted to see you this morning, first thing."

Max said, "I'm glad you did. It gives me the chance to congratulate you firsthand."

"Thanks. I appreciate that, but it's not why I wanted to see you. The fact is that turnkey drilling deal is going to cost me a lot of money, and I'm not happy about it."

"But you certainly understood the deal when you made it, and you knew why I had to do it that way. As I told you, I can't have overcalls with these investors. It's out of the question. They pull a switch themselves, sometimes, but nobody pulls it on them."

"Yes, you did tell me that. I agree."

"And I also told you that I had to be in on precisely the same terms as my et als, didn't I?"

"You did. But you're really an 'industry partner' by now, and that means you should be straight-up with me. Whatever the actual cost is, you should be paying your share, redrilling, recompletion, cleanup, whatever it is."

"Barney, that's not the deal we made. Look at the contract."

"I know what the damn contract says, Max. I'm talking about what's right. You've got a quarter of the well and your et als have a quarter. I understand why they had to be protected against an overcall. But you ought to be paying your quarter working interest share of the total cost, whatever it ends up being. You've probably got a quarter of a discovery you'll make ten, twenty, maybe fifty times your money on. And your investors will do just as well. Why are you sticking me with your share of the overcall? That's not right, and you know it." Barney was barely keeping his voice under control.

Max stayed calm. "Because a deal is a deal in my book."

Barney was quiet for a moment. Finally he said, "If that's your last word on this, Max, it's our last deal, too. Do you want to think that over before you make a final decision?"

"I already have, Barney. But if this is a discovery, and it's as good as you think it is, have your controller send me an accounting for the total well cost and the name of your favorite charity. I'll write them a check for the amount of my 24.5 percent share of the additional costs you paid on the turnkey to me, no questions asked. Have a good day, Dad," and he stood up and walked out of the room leaving an infuriated Barney at the table.

Max spent the day back at his office working on a new project for his seven South Western stores. The head shirtmaker at Carroll & Company had asked for an appointment to discuss a new department for those stores, and Max had agreed to see him along with Landers' top merchandise manager and its location expert. Max typically made the key decisions in both of these areas, but he retained the two experienced professionals because they both had convinced him by performance that they had opinions worth hearing and could implement his decisions efficiently.

The shirt man, who called himself Marty Devlin, was ushered into Max's office in the high-rise tower right on time, shook hands with Max and his executives, and then launched into his pitch. He explained that had learned his trade under his father at Turnbull & Asser in London, and then signed on at Carroll's, when he came to Dallas, as a designer and maker of bespoke "rancher" shirts and jackets, with their yoked shoulders, usually adorned with an embroidered miniature of the rancher's brand on the outer panel of the right front yoke. They were prized possessions throughout the region. He talked earnestly to Duke about the habit many proud, wealthy Texans had of wearing ranch-style, bespoke shirts, jackets, and suits, string ties or pendant lariats, with elaborately tooled, bench-made boots and belts, as everyday and even formal dress. He made the case that at least as many wealthy Texans wore this "real Texas" garb as had any special interest in Max's Mayfair "look."

Max and the shirt man costed up a top-drawer, authentic, bespoke rancher's outfit, and estimated its retail price, using authentic materials and, leaving out the boots, they found it to be in the same price range as Max's top Mayfair suits. They both agreed that the bench-made boots probably worked with either style in Texas, although the bootmaker could undoubtedly make any kind of shoe, assuring a typical total sales check higher than Landers' current substantial average. And they figured the space requirements at not much more than room for two mannequins and a fitter's dummy on the sales floor and a little crowding in the storage areas. Max's executives just listened.

Devlin produced a portfolio of customer recommendations and said that Max was welcome to call the Carroll's shop downtown to speak to the manager or one of the members of the family and anyone else about him, even at the risk of letting them know he might be joining a competitor. Max made some calls, while Devlin was waiting outside, and then called him in to share the good news. Every one of the references praised Devlin. Two of them asked if Max and Devlin needed any equity partners and volunteered their services and their money. Max thought it all sounded a little pat and a perhaps too good, but when he ran the numbers in his head, he calculated that he could add about 40 percent to his bottom line on no significant initial capital investment in his existing stores in the Southwest.

"How much money do you need to get into business at my downtown Dallas shop—you know where that is, I'm sure," he added "And how long would it take you to open in that store?"

"Fifty thousand dollars and sixty days," Devlin said.

"Who owns what?" Max asked.

"All your money?"

"Yes," Max answered.

"How about rent and utilities?"

"Pro rata on the revenues."

"Sixty-forty your way, unless I knock your socks off. Then we adjust."

"No adjustment. Sixty-forty all the way, but you can take your business elsewhere any time you want."

"How about a contract?"

"My lawyer drafts; yours gets to pass on it and have his say."

"Is this the way we're always going to work?"

"As long as you do what you say you're going to do. Of course, we'll argue about some things, but we'll mostly agree and split the difference when we don't."

"You got a deal, Mr. Landers," Devlin said and extended his hand.

"So do you, Mr. Devlin." Max shook the hand. "And I'm Max to you. You call me when you have something to discuss with me, and you call these two gentlemen, or either of them, whenever you need their help."

Max took a check out of the folder in his inside breast pocket, filled it out in seconds, and handed it to Devlin. "You're not going to stand around here waiting until the lawyers catch up with us, are you? You've got work to do, Marty. And I don't expect to be disappointed."

Devlin pocketed the check, gave a little half salute, and hustled out the door.

The merchandiser said, "Max, your problem is you just can't make a decision."

The location expert said, "He can when he's already been thinking about something before it gets to the table."

Max opened his hands signaling total innocence.

The merchandiser hesitated, as if pondering whether to say something.

"What's on your mind?" Max asked him.

"Well, I was just wondering . . ."

"Come on, now. Let's hear it."

"If Devlin has a following at Carroll's and a lot of those customers come to him over here, Carroll's might make a claim that he's misappropriating their business, or that you and Devlin are working together to do that."

Max, as usual, thought about the idea before he spoke. Then he said, "Devlin's got a right to try and better himself, doesn't he? And if he can make a better deal for himself here than he has there, why shouldn't he be allowed to do it? Who's going to tell him he can't?"

"If he takes a copy of his list of clients with him, they could claim he's taking their property and sue you both."

"Get in touch with him and tell him not to take anything with him when he leaves Carroll's. Absolutely nothing. Tell him I said I'll run an ad announcing his new department in our Dallas stores when he's ready to open. His clients will put two and two together when they don't see him at Carroll's and do see the ad we run with no reference to them. Stores don't own their customers. I can't see that they'd have a case."

The lease man shrugged his shoulders and said, "You're the boss. I just thought I should mention it."

"I'm glad you did," said Max. "Now let's get him up and running. pronto."

Most of Devlin's clients at Carroll's did follow him for their yoke shirts, dressy Western wear, and boots, but a good many of them were already Landers's customers. Within a year, Max had Devlin's departments in all of his Texas stores. In another year, all the Landers's stores in the South, Southwest, and Far West featured them, and they were all thriving. Carroll's never sued, presumably on advice of counsel.

From the start, Devlin was learning the whole Landers's operation by osmosis, with some occasional instruction from Max. And it was soon clear that he had broad authority over at least a portion of what was becoming a very substantial, nationwide business and the upscale leader in its field. It was also clear that Devlin had the drive, the talent, and the skills to run it all one day, if Max ever decided to step down.

Max himself had the his oil business to run and had developed an increasing interest in portfolio investments in well managed businesses with strong performance records and publicly traded securities selling at fractions of what they had traded for in the previous decade following "The Crash." Three years after they had met for the first time, Max and Devlin were having dinner at one of Max's clubs and discussing trading Devlin's share of his business for 10 percent of Landers's and a contract to run the whole show as its well-compensated CEO.

They had made the deal before they had finished their entrees. Max said he'd have his lawyer draft the purchase and sale agreement but insisted that Devlin retain his own counsel to represent him. Devlin said he didn't need a lawyer to make a deal with The Duke and wouldn't run the risk of having anybody introduce strain between them by trying to impress him or Max with his negotiating skills. Max told Devlin he appreciated the sentiment, but he wanted Devlin to start getting used to working with lawyers because it was becoming impossible to run a substantial business without having them involved, virtually day to day.

"It's a bloody waste of money," Devlin said.

"It's an investment in your higher education as the CEO of a big business," Max summed up. And they each had counsel through the paperwork stage, although Devlin had asked Max's attorney to recommend a lawyer for him and taken the recommendation. Neither lawyer tried to reshape the deal or overcomplicate it, and they closed in less than a month. Max became nonexecutive chairman of Landers and chairman of the Finance Committee, and Devlin became president and CEO, immediately making two major decisions the day of the closing.

He hired the younger lawyer as vice president and general counsel and instructed him to start the process of listing Landers's common stock on the New York Stock Exchange. Five months later, Landers's shares were the first trade of the day on the NYSE, 100 shares at $20 a share. Max owned 4 million shares, Devlin a million, and the public another million. The stock never traded lower.

DANNY '90 II

AFTER ONE PERFORMANCE, AUDREY AND I WENT TO A PARTY IN THE Village hosted at his gallery by an art dealer who was one of her play's "producers," which meant he had been at least a high five-figure investor in the production, maybe low six. The guests were a mixed group, including the writer, the director and the cast, even some of the backstage people, and almost all of the "producers," and there was excitement in the air about the proposed move to Broadway.

I had left Audrey momentarily with several of the actors and stepped over to the bar to refill her white wine and my scotch, and as I waited for the barman to top them up, a very handsome, rather short fellow in what was clearly a designer blazer over an elegant black turtleneck struck up a conversation with "That is an extraordinarily beautiful woman, and evidently yours. I congratulate you," in Parisian-accented perfect English, raising his glass to me.

"Thank you," I said, knowing exactly whom he meant. "She is my fiancée," raising my glass back to him.

"I notice," he went on, "that you've been looking carefully at these rather undistinguished paintings," gesturing around the walls with his highball glass in hand. "Are you a collector?"

"On a very modest scale," I said.

"May I ask what you think of them?"

"At the risk of some unkindness to my host, I must say not much," I answered.

"Further evidence of your good taste," he said, with a contained smile, again lifting his glass to me.

I nodded at him, smiled an apology for not being able to offer a handshake, and walked back to bring Audrey her wine, still carrying my drink in the other hand. The conversation around Audrey was intensely animated and focused on the potential breakthrough Broadway would mean for the cast and the director. That was clearly all they wanted to talk about at the moment, and I drifted away to take a longer look at the pictures, feeling a bit guilty that I had dismissed them, not so much out of concern for the painter, whom I didn't know, but because I did know the dealer, who'd been agreeable on the few prior occasions when we'd met and appeared to be respectful of the fact that Audrey was "otherwise engaged," as not very many of her apparent admirers seemed prepared to be.

Then the French dealer was at my side again. "I understand you are an attorney," he said, "and that you are a securities law litigator among other specialties in Manhattan."

"You're well informed, Monsieur," I said, "and your English is impeccable, if I may say so."

"You may, indeed. Thank you. And you pronounce 'monsieur' as if your French passes muster, as well, Monsieur L'Avocat."

I lifted my glass again to him and told him he was very kind.

"May I ask you what are some of the other areas of the law in which you specialize?"

"Corporate law is my primary field, as a litigator, and I do a good deal of work in mergers and acquisitions." I automatically reached to take a business card out of my jacket pocket and offer it to him.

He pocketed mine and proffered his, which I scanned briefly and put in my pocket. It read simply, Alain Raval, Counseileur Prive, with an address on Avenue Foch and a telephone number.

"Do you by any chance know Danny Miller?" he asked, with "Danny" slightly French, as with one "n" and an "i."

"Doesn't everyone, these days?" I asked.

"Do you?"

I had not yet answered. Audrey called, faux plaintive, "Peter. You've abandoned me!"

I opened my hands, signaling submission, said it had been a pleasure to meet him, half-saluted, and turned, heading back to her.

"I shall call you," Raval said over my back.

And the next morning, just before ten, he did. His first question, after a pleasant greeting, was "Do you represent Miller?"

I assured him I didn't.

"Then you are able to advise me on something that involves him?"

"My position has been that I can't."

"You have been asked the question before?"

"For the same reasons, I don't think I can answer that."

"I studied in the law faculty at the Sorbonne," he said, "although I have never, as you say, 'practiced.' And our system, as you know, is quite different from yours, in any event. But I cannot imagine that you are prohibited from hearing what I might have to say before you decide."

"Are you familiar with our concept of attorney-client privilege?" I asked him.

"To a certain extent," he told me.

I then explained that if we agreed that he was consulting me as his attorney, even if I waived the fee for this interview, anything we discussed would be privileged, and we could not be required to reveal it, except in extraordinary circumstances I was confident would not develop. But I reserved the right to interrupt and stop him if I felt the privilege or my own position might be compromised.

He agreed, and as at least my client pro tem, he began to tell me his story.

"Miller has been my client for some years. The relationship began with him, having been introduced to me by a mutual acquaintance, asking me to buy certain works of art for him, at auction. After satisfying myself as to his financial capabilities and reputation, I made several significant purchases for him, following his desire that I actually buy the works he wanted, and then, after some period of time, resell them to him at a small markup. The works, over time, tended to be more and more costly to buy, and even the small markup I added became a significant source of profit to me.

"Then one day, when we met for lunch in Paris, Danny asked me if I ever invested or traded in American securities. I told him that I did, from time to time, do so. And then he asked me, if he were to guarantee me against loss, would I buy in my own name certain stocks that he directed me to buy with the understanding that I would cause the shares to be voted as he directed me to vote them. Then he added the further proviso that in addition to covering any losses I might incur on those purchases, or occasionally short sales he directed me to make, I would be permitted to keep half of any profits I made on these 'investments.'

"When I asked him how we would, under such an arrangement, as you say, 'settle' our accounts, he said we would do so by adjusting the prices on the artworks I bought at his direction. Then when I asked about the amount of capital I might have to employ in this 'side venture' with him, he told me that one of his 'entities' would arrange a credit line with a French bank, or the Paris office of a foreign bank, to meet my requirements without any obligation on my part, other than, of course, to do his bidding. It was an arrangement very similar, in essence, to what I was doing for him in his capacity as an art collector."

I smiled at that characterization, then sat back in my desk chair and touched my fingertips together before I spoke. "Not exactly," I finally said.

"Shall I go on?" Raval asked.

"No," I said, "I think that's enough for now."

"But, there is much more to tell," he said, "and then I have to ask you some questions."

"I'm sure there is," I told him. "Nevertheless, I now have to think about whether I want to hear it and whether I can give you any advice on it."

"How long do you have to think it over before we can continue?"

I told him I would get back to him the following morning and asked him where I could contact him. He said I could reach him at the St. Regis. We stood up and shook hands, and I escorted him out to the reception area where we parted.

I walked back to my office feeling I knew still more than I wanted to know about the games Danny was playing at the time and the stakes he was playing for. What I didn't know was what I was going to do about it.

Audrey was at the theater that night, and I brought in some sandwiches for a late supper when she came home. Then I poured myself a double scotch, tuned in CBS news on the television in our little library, and sat down to catch up with the day's developments. We had some mixed nuts in a glass dish on the cocktail table, and I had eaten them all and finished my drink by the time the news broadcast was over. Then I took advantage of the time alone to consider what to do about Danny.

I wasn't surprised to have learned that he was up to more market activities that were at least technically illegal. There were already some regulations in place requiring an investor who was buying stock in a publicly traded company to report his purchases and total holdings if he was accumulating the stock with a view to a move for control or even if the play turned into "greenmail." And Danny's actions, taken together, appeared to be aimed in one of those directions. But the regulatory framework was still pretty loose, and there were still no cases directly on point. Besides, I had no adverse client interest to protect, and Danny's counsel was tough and smart. If I made a run at Miller on some loosely defined "public interest" count, the lawyer would probably say I had no right to talk to his client without him, and he could embarrass me with my partners-to-be on those grounds.

I could talk to his lawyer, again, alone, but I was reasonably certain, after our last exchange, that he would brush me off, probably with a warning. On the other hand, if what I suspected proved to be true, it wasn't out of the question that the information I had from various sources might be construed, if a proxy fight did develop, as placing me under some sort of whistle-blowing obligation, at last in the eyes of an overzealous regulator or prosecutor, of my former stripe, with the advantage of hindsight.

Just before Audrey arrived, I concluded I ought to talk with two of our older partners, preferably together, one, Arthur Barden, who already knew Danny, and the other our top securities law litigator and "rainmaker," Judge Farkas, who was considered to be in the

Wachtel, Lipton, Flom league and pretty deeply committed to seeing me assume his mantle, in time. With that much resolved, I turned on some Mozart and set out to finish the Wahloo police procedural I was reading.

The next morning I dropped into Arthur's office, gave him a brief summary of my dilemma, and asked him if he could set up a meeting with Farkas for the three of us at their early convenience. He'd had that brush with Danny a few months before and was obviously curious. We met late that afternoon.

They both heard me out and, after some intelligent questions, agreed with my suspicions that Danny was probably planning a surprise takeover bid for the pharmaceutical company and, again, probably, already over the line on reporting. The two of them were also in agreement on what I could do, and that was nothing. The litigator, the commanding Judge Farkas, who was the de facto head of the firm, put it bluntly to close the meeting, "I don't see that we have a dog in that fight. So we'd better stay out and keep mum."

I had less than two months to go before the partnership was voted on and offered to me. I had no blots in my copybook and no appetite for a tangle with Danny Miller that could end up as one. Out I stayed, through the end of the year, through the invitation, my acceptance, the celebratory partners' dinner, and the Christmas Eve through New Year's Day holiday Audrey and I took at Sandy Lane, in Barbados.

I was back in the office on the third, and my new room with a view had been freshly done up over the previous two weeks, my personal possessions moved in over the holiday week. The firm had kept its commitment, and I was comfortable with my partners and my place among them. I was, I felt confident, well positioned and ready for whatever came in the door. But I was not prepared for the first call that Wednesday morning.

"Peter," Danny said, "congratulations. I never had any doubts that you'd be there with a great firm, but it's nice to see it happen so soon. And I'd like to meet with you right away. I'll come over to your office. How's eleven o'clock?"

I told him I appreciated the call, but I had a meeting starting before eleven and running into the afternoon that I couldn't miss. He said he could make it late afternoon, and it was clear he would keep punching until I conceded I could make some time before midnight. We settled on five. I knew it was going to be about what I had told Farkas and Barden I'd like to avoid. But corporate lawyers make time to hear out potential clients who pay seven figure legal fees.

Danny was right on time. I picked him up in the reception room on my floor and walked him back to my office. He stood admiring the "cityscape" spread river to river below my angle in the curtain wall "corner office" and said, "Very, very nice. Peter. I'm happy for you, and I know you deserve it. I'll sit here," and took the window side of the couch.

"Thanks. Can I get you some coffee?"

"No," he said. "I'm fine. I know it's late, and I appreciate your making the time. Let's get right to business."

"Let's go," I said, sat down behind my desk and turned the chair to face him.

"You've probably guessed it, Peter, because I happen to know you've been given enough hints."

"Why don't you tell me anyway, Danny, then I won't have to guess."

"OK. We'll do it your way. I think somebody downtown has decided to come after me for allegedly violating reporting rules on some recent stock purchases," he said.

"Downtown?"

"I think it's the U.S. Attorney on a referral from the SEC. I think they're also working with the Manhattan DA's office and maybe the state AG."

"That's a lot of muscle for a reporting violation."

"I'm a pretty prominent player, as you know, and knocking me off would make enough headlines to jump-start a political career or two."

"You've already got a very good securities lawyer, Danny. What do you need me for?"

"You know he's a pretty arrogant guy, and I ruffle enough feathers myself. I don't need a lawyer who has his own collection of people with scores to settle."

"I'm not the most popular guy in town, Danny. Every prosecutor put somebody's son away unjustly, according to the family. In my case, it's a pretty long list, considering how long, or short, depending on your point of view, I was on the job."

"Peter," he said, with a big smile, "the word is that you're the best lawyer in this town, doing this kind of work."

"You've got to be kidding, Danny. I'm in private practice for just less than one year. I'm not even on the screen. Guys like you would ordinarily need a scorecard and a number on my back to know who the hell I am. So would you if we hadn't gone to school together."

"Peter, let's not dance to this. You're modest. I appreciate that. It's a lovely quality in a gentleman. But what you did as a prosecutor counts. You're also a hard-nosed SOB, which I happen to know from personal experience. If anybody can make this go away quietly, it's you. So that's why I'm here. Bearing gifts, and I'm sure you know what I mean."

"We still bill me at $400 an hour this year. Same rate to you and everybody else. And I keep straight books. So don't wave big money at me. That's your game, not mine."

"And you hate my guts, with good reason. So you don't really want my money, right? But let me ask you, what would your partners think if you told me to take a walk?"

"I'd like to believe they'd think that was my business."

"You have to know it doesn't work that way. Rich clients don't get turned away unless they're child molesters, if then, Peter. My money is as good as anybody else's. And I know you're not going to tell me I'm not entitled to the best representation I can get."

"Danny, we have a miserable history together. There are plenty of good lawyers in town who're not on many enemies' lists and probably don't feel any animus toward you, as you know I do. You don't need me, and I don't need you. Why push this?"

"You know enough about me to realize I generally get what I want. I don't stop until I do. In this instance, I want you as my lawyer, whatever it costs. And you will be my lawyer, Peter. Whether we agree on that today or tomorrow or the next day. So why waste time? I'll give you all the facts. You string them together and make a winning defense out of them. You can do it. I can pay for it. It's a perfectly fair arrangement. Let's just do it."

"Danny Miller, you wouldn't know what was fair if it hit you in the head. In fact, I did try to hit you in the head once, with perfect justification, and it taught you absolutely nothing. Fairness is not measured in financial equivalents. It's a matter of ethics, of which I know you have none."

"And what about you, Peter? If you really wanted to apply your own ethical standard to the question of whom you'd represent and whom you wouldn't, you should have gone into practice for yourself, not joined a firm knowing you'd never give your partners a shot at making that decision and probably not even tell them about what you'd done. That's not ethical, by any standard I know. It's self-serving and vindictive, but it sure isn't treating your partners fairly.

"Ethically, if you'll excuse my daring to express myself in your area of special expertise, your behavior is shit."

"You don't think my partners would back me?"

"I sure don't. I'm not some ax murderer. I don't even take money from widows and orphans. I'm a guy who can make money and pay big fees, without breaking the law. You want to ask your partners if they want to send me to the firm on the next six floors. Be my guest. But at least give them a vote. If they choose to represent me, do the right thing. Take the case. If they vote to tell me to take a walk, I'm gone. You have my word on that."

"Your word?" I asked, with some bite.

"Yeah, Peter. My word. Did you ever see me break it?"

"That's a little narrow, Danny, for my taste."

"That's what my business is built on. A man's word."

"From one bandit to another, that's what your business is based on."

"It's been good enough for a long time."

"Sure," Peter said, "as long as it pays well."

"You know you really are a self-righteous prig, Peter."

"Let's keep to the issues, Danny. I won't represent you. That's it."

"Because I fucked your girlfriend?"

I lunged around the desk to get my hands on him. Danny swept up the marble paperweight on the corner of the desk and cracked it against my forehead in one astonishingly quick motion. I sank to the floor, bleeding, and blacked out. I woke up in the emergency room at St. Vincent's with Audrey sitting beside my bed, holding my hand. The first thing I thought of was how fast Danny's hand had moved to take me out. No hesitation, just a blur, and then a blow, and lights out.

*   *   *

"How do you feel, darling?"

"I'm pretty groggy. But OK, thanks. The light is a little bright for me, so I'm going to keep my eyes closed, love. But we can talk. I'm up to it."

She touched my cheek, then kissed me very gently on the lips. "You may fall asleep, and don't worry about it. They were waking you almost ever hour last night until I left, and I don't think you got much sleep."

"Maybe. We'll see."

"Can you tell me what actually happened? The story is you were attacked by a client."

"The other way around. I had a meeting with Danny Miller, and it turned hostile. I actually attacked him, although you may find that incredible. But Danny hit me with something hard from my desk, and that's all I remember. He is one quick, tough little bastard, and I guess I forgot that in the heat of the exchange. I let him get under my skin, and he got the better of it. That's all I can tell you. It's a good thing he hit me in the hardest part of my head, or I could have been badly hurt, and it would have been my own fault."

"You did get hurt. You were seriously concussed, and it took twelve stitches to close the split across your forehead. But you really were lucky, I guess. It could have been worse."

"Was anyone from my office here?"

"Your assistant found you, after Miller left, apparently in a big hurry. She called for the ambulance and checked on you through the evening and again early this morning. One of your partners wants to come over as soon as you're up to it. I said I'd call him."

"Who?"

"Emile Farkas."

"The great man himself?"

"Shall I call him?"

"Not just yet. I'd like to think about what I'm going to say."

"Well, he said when you're up to it. I don't think there's any rush."

I lay back with my eyes closed. After a while I asked her if she was planning to go on that night.

"I guess so," she said. "If you're not in any danger."

"I'm sure I'm not. He's certainly not going to attack while I'm lying here in the hospital."

"I meant from what he's already done. You really did have a serious concussion and a head wound. Your doctor has no intention of releasing you today. You may be here a couple of days until they've thoroughly checked you out."

I thought for a minute, then I said there was no point in exasperating the judge. "You can call him now and tell him I'm up to seeing him. It will take him a few minutes to get here anyway. I'll have my version rehearsed when he does."

"Will I be able to listen?" she asked.

"I'd really rather tell it just once, but I think I should talk to him alone. I'll give you the blow-by-blow when you come in tomorrow."

"And in the interim?"

"You just don't know until I tell you."

"It makes me look like some featherbrain."

"No, just a good wife giving me a chance to get my wits back before you press me for the ugly details."

"OK." She picked up the bedside telephone and dialed my office receptionist, asked for Judge Farkas, announced herself to his assistant, and when he came on the line, told him very graciously that I was looking forward to seeing him anytime. Then thanked him and rang off.

"He'll be here in about half an hour," she said. "And I'm going to go home and get a few minutes' rest before I go to the theatre, OK?" Even with next to no sleep, she looked exquisite.

"Sure," I said. She kissed me gently again and wished me luck with the judge, then slipped out of the room.

I told her, as she left, not to worry, that Farkas was a big booster of mine and really a friend. It would go OK today, and I would undercut anything self-serving Danny might say later. She gave me a thumbs-up. I did fall asleep again, and when I awoke, the judge was sitting in the chair next to my bed.

"I'm glad to hear you're coming around, and that's the report at the nurses' station," he said.

"Thanks. It's good of you to come by."

"Are you up to talking?"

"I think so."

Farkas was a very confident man. He knew what he wanted to know, and, very politely, he went right after it. "Well, you stop when you feel any strain, but I'm anxious to know exactly what happened yesterday."

"Briefly, Danny Miller, whom I've known since secondary school, asked me late yesterday to represent him in what will probably be a substantial effort to take over Wyco, which, as I'm sure you know, is a medium-sized Big Board drug and medical equipment company. I happen to know, from other sources, some of the details of how he is operating below the reporting radar, so far, in putting together a control block he owns beneficially or directly.

"Those details known to me indicate that he is probably required both to announce his plan and make appropriate announcements of his position and changes in it as they take place. I assure you I have made no effort to solicit this information, which has been provided to me voluntarily by parties seeking my advice, and I have so far not accepted any of the offers to be retained to advise any of those parties potentially adverse to Miller because I might be arguably conflicted, for various reasons.

"Late yesterday afternoon, Miller came to my office at the firm to ask me to represent him in his takeover effort. I refused, for what I believe to be valid legal ethics grounds , and Miller was very unhappy, claiming, or at least implying, strongly that my stance denied him proper representation, because of my personal animus toward him. He essentially threatened to appeal to my partners to overrule me, presumably because of his readiness to pay very large fees to the firm if I did represent him.

"There is also another conflict. Arthur Barden has done T&E work for the younger brother of the Wyco CEO and largest shareholder. Arthur would have to tell you himself how extensive his relationships are with the family. He brought the younger brother in for a consultation with me some months ago, and we represented that brother in his sale of part of his Wyco stake to Miller, with Danny taking an option from our client on the rest of his stock.

"Subsequently, a put and call broker I know came to me for advice on how to handle the risky position Danny had put him in by insisting that he sell, with Danny's guaranteeing him against loss, what was in proportion to his firm's capital a major volume of puts on Wyco to clients Miller referred to him. This fellow had been a classmate and teammate of Danny's and mine at school, but he had sought me out on his own, not on Danny's referral. And he was very worried that he'd be unable to cover if all the puts he'd sold on Danny's guarantee ever fell in on him and Danny didn't honor the guarantee. I turned him away, too, on the potential conflict grounds, converting an old, if not very close, friend into an angry enemy.

"I also learned, inadvertently, that Miller is using a French private art dealer to buy Wyco stock as a beard, with Danny arranging a put for him with the same P&C broker, in an elaborate deal, again substantially guaranteeing the art dealer/beard against loss."

"How do you know all this?"

"Both the art dealer and the P&C broker came to me for advice about Miller. But so far, I haven't agreed to represent either of them or billed out any of my time with them."

The judge shifted his position to get the light out of his eyes. "Now I'd like to know exactly what happened last night between you and the hotshot," he finally said.

"Danny called me early in the day and asked to see me on business right away. I tried to dissuade him, because there had been some substantial hostility between us since we were roommates at Yale, and I really had no desire to represent him despite his widely reported success. Let's say I had good grounds not to trust him from the last picture, even if I were prepared to withhold judgment on his current activities until I heard his side of the stories. But he insisted, and I agreed to see him. I was booked solid until 5 p.m., and we made the appointment, at Connelly, for then.

"I escorted him into my office and offered him a chair to the right of my desk. We had a testy conversation in which I did not repeat what I had been told about his 'operations,' but made it clear that I wasn't prepared to represent or advise him. He threatened me with going to my partners to complain that I was turning away important new business because of some petty grudge I'd held against him for years.

"I told him I'd arrange an appointment for him to lodge his complaint with the proper parties at the firm. Then, I guess, seeing he was getting nowhere with me and very irritated about not getting his own way—and knowing me from way back when—he found the right button to push with me, maybe the only one that would have had his intended effect. He said something he knew was absolutely infuriating.

"You know me. You know I'm cool under fire. That's a reputation I've earned and prized. But the fact is he knew exactly how to get to me and did. I came out of my chair ready to bounce him off the wall. Not that I didn't know how tough that little bastard is. I'd watched him win the NCAA's his sophomore year at Yale. And every other wrestling competition he'd ever entered. I must outweigh him by sixty pounds. But I wasn't making a calculus. I just blew, and he did his number, snatching some marble piece off my desk and in the same sweep, cracking it against my forehead before I even got a hand on him. The next thing I knew, I was waking up in the emergency room. I'm not even sure how much later, or how I got there."

"Peter, I want to be entirely clear on this. You physically attacked him, in your office, to which he had come for the purpose of asking you to represent him?"

My headache returned with almost blinding intensity. I closed my eyes for a moment and waited for it to ease up. It didn't. Finally I said, "That's the essence of it. Yes."

"I can't believe it."

"Judge, you'd have to know the full story."

"If I did, would that change these specific facts?"

I fought the wooziness that followed the pain in my head.

"Mitigate them, perhaps, in some degree. But change them? No. It happened, as I've said."

Farkas leaned back in the chair at my bedside, running his hand through his gleaming white hair. "Christ, Peter, what would you do in my position?" he asked.

"I don't know, Judge. It was an inexcusable lapse of control on my part. I lost it. I let Miller provoke me, knowing even at the moment that was exactly what he wanted to do. How does a responsible adult who's a partner in a major law firm allow that to happen? It's like something out of an O'Hara novel. Do you want me to resign?"

The judge stood up and snapped, "Hell, no! Where would that get us? Let me think a minute, and you do the same if you're up to it. And by the way, it may sound a bit cavalier to you, since you're the one lying in bed with your head split, but it's a damn good thing you're the party injured and not he."

"You're right, Judge. I've been thinking that myself."

"So it could be worse. Console yourself with that. Meanwhile, I'm going to walk around the block or the hall, whatever, and give myself a chance to think."

I lay back and tried to think, but I couldn't focus. I just lay still, with my eyes closed, and tried to breathe regularly, half asleep, until Farkas came back into the room.

"I have a plan," he said, standing at the end of my bed.

That snapped me back into focus. "Let's hear it, Judge."

"As soon as you can do it, you call Miller, at his home or his office, whichever feels right to you. Tell him you lost your head over whatever it was between you that presumably he knows as well as you do. But you've cooled down, and you realize we can give him better representation than anybody else, and you and I are going to work together on it. You'll be first chair, and I'll assist. We'll do it jointly. He does know who I am, doesn't he?"

"I assume anybody in his position does," I assured him. "But I think we should reverse the seating assignments. I wouldn't feel comfortable leading you."

"But you will lead. That's my decision. I am only there so he knows he's not going to be sold out. He'll get the best representation money can buy. You tell him that. And by the way, what the hell has he done that has him so concerned? Do you know?"

"I know just enough to be reasonably sure he's mounting a hostile takeover move against a major company and going about it, at least in part, by doing some things that are of questionable legality if not clearly illegal. The regs and the law have been moving, in fits and starts, toward requiring early disclosure of plans like that, and he's way out of line on the strength of what I know, which is probably just a fraction of what he's doing."

"On what you know, and I realize that's limited, is he a lost cause? Can we give him a realistic defense?"

"Given the state of the regs, the Exchange rules, and the law at the moment, I'm pretty sure we can. The point is, do we want to?"

"Besides your personal animus toward him, is there any reason we should turn down a significant fee to do so?"

"Maybe primarily that he's a very, very bad guy who wouldn't hesitate to do just about anything to win. But it's also true that I've been a leader in the movement to tighten the rules on takeover behavior, and it's going to be a disappointment to some very good people who've been working with me for reform to see me helping a prime offender get away with what we've been fighting to stop."

"Is he really any worse than the rest of the raiders?"

"I won't know until we put some more facts together. But he's certainly not the only very bad boy operating in the markets these days. The cover is 'shareholders rights,' or in the business school journal articles, 'creative destruction.' What that usually really means is asset stripping, labor force reductions, and raider enrichment."

The judge gripped the bedstead hard enough to turn his knuckles white. "You understand, Peter, I'm sure, that we do not have to win his case, if he really has committed an actionable offense. But we do have to give him the best defense we can. And if we win the case for him, that's how it goes. We give it our absolute best shot, agreed?"

"If he's as bad as I believe him to be, as I know him to be in some respects, should we be taking his case?"

"That's our business. That's our responsibility."

"To abet his activities?"

"To defend him to the best of our ability."

"And take the fees."

"Of course."

"The bigger the better."

"Absolutely."

"Even if we make it tougher to regulate the industry."

"That's right."

"It doesn't feel so right."

"Listen, Peter. Either you're in or you're out. But he pays for the best we can give him, and he gets it. I came off the federal appellate bench to make some real money in private practice. And I like doing that. I did my public service, to the very best of my ability, twenty-five years plus, and I see to it that we do more than our share of pro bono work, every year. But my professional duty now dictates that I serve my clients' legitimate interests. So does yours."

"I note the qualifying adjective."

"Peter, in this instance, we're not going to put too fine a point on that. Are we clear?"

"You're the judge," I said.

"No, I'm not. Not any more. And especially not in this instance. I'm Danny Miller's advocate, and so are you. Are we clear on this?

If we're not, say so now, Peter, and we'll find some other way to deal with whatever we have to. Tell me now, Peter, or forever hold your peace."

"As you know, Judge, I'm not at my best right now. I should think it over, overnight."

"Peter, partner, you've got half an hour. I'll take another walk around the block and come back for your answer."

He did, and I gave him what he wanted. I called Danny at his office that afternoon and told him my decision, with no apologies. I did assure him he would get my best efforts and the judge's. Danny said he was "sorry" he said what he said and hoped I was recovering quickly. He "understood" why I had flown off the handle. But no harm, no foul, the son-of-a-bitch.

I rang and asked the nurse for a sedative, which she would not give me, in my condition. I still fell asleep, and the nurses didn't wake me. I finally did, myself, and found my wife lying beside me, on top of the blanket cover, getting a little nap before her evening performance. I lay still, keeping my breathing slow and steady, not to wake her.

MAX '32-'39

MAX AND BETSY WERE PEOPLE WHO COULD HANDLE THE INEVITABLE disputes in business, but had no real appetite for them at home. It was nearly impossible to agree on everything and with their mutual antipathy toward slugging it out, they developed a routine that worked for them. If there was an issue on which they weren't almost immediately in agreement, they would make the time to sit down over a drink or two, preferably before dinner, at home, and talk it out.

Generally, they traded "what do you thinks," and one of them said, "You know you're right, let's do it that way." If they didn't get there in the time it took to down two drinks apiece, Max would usually suggest they sleep on it, or think about it, and put the decision off for a day or two, then try again. They really did not go through "a period of adjustment." They were lucky enough to like and respect each other from the start, and they both knew it would take an extraordinarily divisive issue to warrant a serious disagreement.

The first time Max asked her about having children was toward the end of their second year together. Betsy said she thought she would like at least another year of the life they were enjoying without that responsibility, if it was all right with him. The next time they discussed the subject she had brought it up. It was just about a year later.

"If you're ready, I am," she said one evening while they were out for dinner alone at a favorite restaurant.

"I'm sorry, darling. Ready for what was that?"

"Babies," she said.

121

"What did you say?"

"I say we put the program in motion tonight. That's what I say, Mr. Landers."

It took a little over eighteen months, with one early and briefly disheartening miscarriage, but Betsy gave birth to a healthy girl who looked as an infant as if she might grow up to be as beautiful as her mother. They named her Dorothea after her maternal grandmother and agreed to wait a while before trying for the matched pair. They had been able to enlist Betsy's own nurse who had been thinking of retiring but was delighted to delay that plan, join their household, and see the baby off to a proper start.

Then, as if in a blink, it was the spring of 1939, and, for most Americans, nearing the end of a grim decade. But Betsy and Max had sailed through, working hard, playing hard, rich, getting steadily richer, aware of their exceptional circumstances and occasionally warning each other not to take them for granted. Betsy rode regularly, but had stopped jumping. She played a lot of tennis, very well, and some golf, got Dorothy up on a pony not too long after she could walk, and had her in ballet classes, tennis lessons, and piano lessons, as often as possible, with Betsy in the mix, nearly every waking moment.

Max left the instructions to his wife, but crammed in a lot of tender attention to his daughter, between running his now very large businesses and pursuing his new passion, golf, whenever he could manage it. It was the first organized sport he'd ever been involved in, and he brought the same intensity of focus to it that he had to making his fortune. Playing no more than once a week, but practicing nearly every day for brief, disciplined periods, he was playing to a ten handicap in two years, getting to be known as the toughest five in town a year later.

He had a putting green and a pitching area installed on the two building lots they'd purchased on either side of their home, and he could putt "lights out" on Bermuda, bent, or macadam, especially with money on the line. It never seemed to bother him to be one of only three Jewish members of his golf club. It did, however, bother some of the other members when he won the club championship at thirty-eight, five years after he first picked up a club.

Nor did he pay much attention at first to the stories about persecution of Jews in Germany after Hitler came to power. Max had grown up with European anti-Semitism as a boy, dealt with a share of it even as he rose to prominence in business in the U.S., and just considered it a harsh fact of life that Jews had to learn to handle. But by the fall of 1938, the stories out of Germany were more than simply reflections of an age-old problem. The reports of Kristallnacht that November were, he recognized, just the vanguard of the horrors to be inflicted on millions of victims with whom he increasingly found himself identifying—his people—wherever they lived or suffered and died, in Diaspora.

Then just months later, when Nazi armies invaded Poland and the British, the French, and the Belgians announced that the invasion meant they, too, were at war with Germany, Max knew what these events taking place thousands of miles away from Dallas made inevitable. This was going to be America's war, too, he knew with sickening certainty. And for him, for Max Landers, the man who had made, with his wits and his bare hands, a safe and bountiful world for himself, his wife, and his daughter, it was already his war. He could feel it in his Jewish bones.

He couldn't readily discuss it at the country club, or the Petroleum Club, or with his oil partners, but he did begin attending the one free-standing synagogue in the city, perhaps the only public place in town where the outrages against the Jews in Germany were openly discussed. And for the first time since he came to America, he found himself acutely aware of his differentiation from almost all of the people around him on the highways every day, in the stores on weekdays and Saturdays, and in the ubiquitous churches on Sundays.

Listening to the news on the radio mornings and evenings, reading the local newspapers, overhearing snatches of conversation in the places he frequented, he also became fully aware, for the first time, of the profoundly isolationist attitudes of his fellow citizens and the depth of their belief that European Jews, their afflictions and their fates, were not Americans' concern. After a week of deliberation, he felt he had to discuss his anguish and what he proposed to do about it with Betsy.

"Haven't we enough troubles in our own country these days, Max?" she asked. "After ten years of the worst Depression in our history, millions still out of work, banks failing, businesses closing, people hungry, homeless, angry, depressed. If you want to do something to help relieve suffering, can't you do it right here?"

"I can, and I do. I write checks for good causes all the time, but that's not the same thing as what I'm talking about."

"What more can you do at your age but write checks? And it's wonderful that you do what you do."

"Thanks. And I'll continue to do it. But there's something else I feel I have to do, too. I have to try to get Jews while they're still alive out of Germany and Eastern Europe and into this country or wherever else they can live in peace. I've got to try."

"If you feel that strongly, then I guess you have to do it, if you can."

"I might have to go where they are, first find out where they are, the people in danger, and then go there to work it out."

"That's really looking for trouble. I don't think you ought to do that. You should work from this country and through people who are already in those places or have access to them. You can't just run around Europe trying to get started from scratch where you're not known, where you don't have contacts. It could be dangerous, and it could be a waste of time."

"A waste of time trying to save the lives of innocent people? Even if I failed it would never be a waste of time. I've got to try."

"I'm sorry. I didn't mean it would be 'a waste of time' trying to save lives. What I meant was that you might not be able to get anything done, now that there's a real war on in Europe, and you could be risking the danger to yourself with no chance of accomplishing what you want to do. Will you at least investigate the situation from here?"

Max said he would, and did. A week later he told Betsy that he had learned his best bet was to go to London, where he knew of some wealthy Jews who were already trying to do what he proposed and possibly go to Switzerland where he could find intermediaries who might help him. She could see his determination and decided to drop her opposition. Max left on a Pan Am flight to London departing from New York three days later. He did send a telegram on arrival at Croydon saying he had landed safely and missed Betsy and Dorothea terribly already. Then . . . nothing.

His partner, Devlin, was of Irish descent but born and raised in London, where he'd apprenticed and ultimately worked as a bespoke tailor and shirtmaker at Turnbull. He had contacts at most levels of society, including Oxford and Cambridge Firsts of distinguished lineage, now in the Foreign Ministry, War Office, and admiralty, whom he'd "dressed" as a young fitter at the Royal Patent haberdasher.

Through them, he managed to have Max traced as far as the French side of the Pyrenees where the trail went cold. His sources said their best surmise was that Max had been taken for a spy and killed by Nazi agents. All the way through the Second World War, Betsy believed Max was alive and would find his way back to her when he could. But the scant evidence turned up by a very extensive and costly effort left Betsy the only believer in that forlorn hope, and even she realized in time that she was simply dismissing facts she could not bear to accept.

*   *   *

About three years after Max's disappearance, a man named Marchetti appeared at her office, presented an engraved calling card, and asked to see her on a personal matter, identifying himself as an old friend of her husband. She hesitated a bit, fearing some sort of a scam when her secretary described him as very well dressed, maybe a little too well by local standards, but a bit rough spoken for all his quiet good manners and respectful demeanor. But the very idea of being able to talk about Max with someone who claimed to know him well was ultimately irresistible to her, and they were soon seated a few feet apart around a conference table in her office as Betsy poured coffee and asked Marchetti how he took his.

"Black, one sugar, thanks," he said, frankly staring at her as she spooned the small cube into his cup, picked up her own, and sat back, pressing her knees demurely together. He was still holding his fedora on his left knee with his left hand as he took the coffee from her with his right.

He caught himself and immediately apologized, with evident embarrassment, for gazing at her so intently, as if he had suddenly realized his look could easily be misinterpreted. "I was just amazed by how beautiful you are, really not like anybody else I've ever seen, except on a movie screen. I'm sorry if I gave you the wrong idea. Believe me."

"Please don't be uncomfortable. I'm actually very flattered. And please tell me how you know my husband."

"That's a long story, Mrs. Landers. Let's just say he kind of worked for me a bit when he was a youngster, pretty much a greenhorn, new to this country, just starting out. And I came to like him, a lot. In fact, I loved him. I wished he had been my son. And when he grew up and became a big success, it didn't surprise me a bit, because I always knew he was very special. I was a little bit of help to him, in the beginning, maybe more than a little.

"We stayed close, even though I didn't see him, hardly at all. But he always knew I was there for him, if he ever needed me. Which, after a little while, he sure never did, because he always could handle himself, in any situation, and it ended up he helped me a lot more than I ever helped him. So if there's anything you ever need, you can count on me to help. I mean anything. All you have to do is call me at that number on my card, and it's as good as done."

He looked at her sternly. "Do you know what I mean? Anything you need, you've got. Anything you have to have done, it's done. And you don't owe anybody anything back. Do you understand what I'm trying to say?"

"That's very kind of you, Mr. Marchetti. But Max arranged for me to be completely secure until he comes home. My daughter and I have everything we'll ever need while he's away."

"Well, there's one thing I want you to know. Troubles come out of nowhere. You never know, 'til they do. They're just there suddenly. I'm here to tell you, if you ever have any, you call me, and myself and other friends of The Duke will make them go away." He dusted his hands together. "Just like that."

"I'm really very grateful, and I will tell Max how kind you've been."

"That's the other thing I came to tell you, Mrs. Landers. You can only tell The Duke something in your dreams. I know you think he's coming back to you, no matter what people say. And I'm real sorry to have to tell you that's just not so, no way, no how. Myself and some other friends of his are very well connected all over the world. We checked it up, down, and sideways, inside out. Some real bad people disappeared our great guy, right in the prime of his life. They're gonna pay for doing that terrible thing someday, because we never forget, and we always balance our books. But that's our business. Your business is to know he's gone and get on with your life and let me know if you ever need anything."

He stood, brushing a tear from his dark circled right eye. "It never hurt me so much to say anything in my life. But you've got to move on. And I know that's exactly what Max would want me to tell you." He backed out of her office, like a courtier retreating from his sovereign's presence, then turned at the door and walked purposefully down the corridor, and, as far as Betsy ever knew, out of her life.

She sat for a few minutes, ignoring her calls, wondering what kind of relationship Max could have had with the rough-voiced gangster who was offering her his protection and what knowledge he could possibly have about Max's death. Maybe he knew because he had special means of accessing the facts. Maybe he had had a hand in Max's fate. In any case, her intuition told her Marchetti did firmly believe Max was dead.

Still having her calls held, she managed to work her way into midafternoon. Then she asked not to disturbed and wept alone, desperately, crushed, shuddering in the unlit room and the gathering dusk, until the sun slipped below the western horizon, taking her hope for the future with it. Then she thought of the child at home waiting anxiously for her mother to walk through the door to her room. She used her private bathroom to wash her face, apply a little makeup, brush her hair, and rush home on the worst day of her life.

She thought, on the way, about what and how to tell Dorothea, and by the time she reached the driveway, she had decided. Marchetti's information was not gospel. His sources were probably criminals who had no better claim to credibility in France than they would have had in Chicago. They said whatever served their interests. Her Max was out there alive. She felt it even now. When the war ended, Max would come home, as she had always known he would. There was no need to tell Dorothea anything else, or to believe it herself.

Years before, when the word had begun to filter back that their agents had lost Max's trail, Devlin and Max's lawyer, the senior Trusts and Estates attorney at what was then still Walker & McGovern, explained to her that two-thirds of Max's significant assets had been transferred immediately before he left to trusts for herself and Dorothea, and the remaining third, in Max's name, bequeathed on his death to a charitable foundation to be managed by Betsy, and, finally, that Betsy, already wealthy by inheritance and a significant earner through her own business efforts, was now extremely rich, even by Texas standards.

They confirmed that Landers was thriving under Devlin's management, that Barney had agreed to manage Max's oil and gas interests along with his own, gratis, of course, and that each of them would welcome as much of a role in management as she cared to take, whenever she chose to take it. She was already a director of Landers, and Devlin offered her the Chair if she wanted it, when she wanted it, assuring her the board would vote as he recommended.

They also told her that they knew nothing and no one could make up for the man she had lost, and when she insisted that he was not lost and would return to her when he could, they each offered to do anything they could for her, at any time, while Max was "away." She left the law firm's conference room alone, at her own insistence, dry-eyed, straight-backed, expressionless, heading directly home to cherish and raise her daughter and wait for her husband's return.

She finished the design contracts she had undertaken, and then turned the practice over to her staff for an indefinite period. Within two months she was going to the office again every day, reclaiming her place as the top interior designer in town while devoting more than half her waking hours to Dorothea.

Devlin was good company and while he certainly did not have Max's apparently instinctive social grace, he did have a wry wit that made her and most of her women friends laugh. The males (except for the homosexuals, all of whom were in the closet), many of whom, especially from the old families, had been reasonably gracious to him when he was fitting their shirts, were not ready to accept Dev as a social equal, despite his success in business, and they generally found him much less amusing. But as a friend and occasional escort for Betsy, he was the beau ideal: bright, increasingly well and broadly informed, never even hinting at romantic aspirations, helpful with Dorothea, Barney, lawyers and accountants, and any kind of business problem. He was the big brother she'd never had, deeply devoted, wholly undemanding, safely married to a woman he loved.

They spent a great deal of time together, leading her father and other members of her set to believe they might be "an item" one day, if not now. But when the war was over, the veterans back home and Max still "missing," it was Devlin who actually brought around a candidate he thought she might consider. The fellow had been a very young Air Corps lieutenant colonel, a double-ace fighter pilot squadron leader briefly stationed at Carswell Air Base outside Ft. Worth, training younger pilots, when Devlin met him and made two uniforms for him in '44.

Glenn Benziger, scion of a family of Chicago bankers, educated at Deerfield and Harvard before the war, had entered the service as a 90-day wonder second lieutenant-to-be and mustered out one of the youngest bird colonels in the air force, a full-fledged hero in Europe, and then again in the Pacific, with a chest full of decorations, including the DFC and a Silver Star, and no fixed idea of where to settle down or what to do when he did. The family banking business was there for him at senior executive levels, but fresh out of uniform, with an independent income and next to no commercial experience, attractive, single, and confident he could make his own way, that option didn't appeal to him much at the time.

Remembering Devlin as a likeable fellow who knew the city and with a few Air Corps buddies to look up, as well, he flew down to Dallas after a week with his family in Chicago and Willamette. Betsy was always reluctant to meet "candidates," "knowing" that Max would come home. But she allowed Devlin to talk her into meeting the young war veteran, and even the unattainable object, the beautiful, successful, superbly connected, effectively single mother wasn't unhappy she'd been persuaded. Glenn, riding since he was four, had been a six-goal polo star before the war, and the morning after they met, Betsy and he were airing her horses out in the countryside, slowing down every few miles to walk them and talk as if they'd grown up together. And despite the thousand miles between their childhood homes they might just as well have. Their hyperprivileged backgrounds had given them easy access to a virtually shared culture. They talked to each other as if they had been doing it all their lives.

Barney, of course, was ecstatic. After learning to deal with Max's heritage and the occasional appearance of an "old friend" of his with hard-bitten features and roughened skin not quite compatible with his Landers tailoring, he soon found Glenn as comfortingly familiar as his favorite boots and reveled in the fact that the younger man looked enough like him to be taken for his son. He rode with them, played golf with them, lunched, drank, and dined with them, and, still careful not to push Betsy too hard on the fact that it would soon be seven years since Max had gone missing, made it clear that Glenn Benziger was a man who rated serious consideration, the perfect son-in-law; why not the perfect husband?

Dorothea was not as easily won over. She was an extraordinarily lovely nine-year-old, intelligent and thoughtful, as polite with Glenn as she was with everyone, but clearly still devoted to the idealized memory of the father she had lost but whose presence she couldn't even remember, and for a cossetted little girl, noticeably subdued. Glenn, who had grown up with a younger brother and a much younger sister, had an easy manner with her and made a continuous, graceful effort to earn her trust and affection, without ever seeming to press. After a slow start, attributable as much to his careful pacing as to her restraint, he made steady progress, as the child saw his determination to fill the hole in her mother's life and her own. Barney consistently made Glenn's case with mother and child, displaying, for him, remarkable sensitivity in the way he went about it.

In less than a month, Glenn was certain he wanted to marry Betsy and adopt Dorothea. Out of respect and affection, he told Barney his intentions over lunch on the clubhouse terrace between nines, just at the zenith of a brilliant fall Sunday. Barney signaled the waiter and asked him to bring over one of the last bottles of his favorite '37 Veuve Clicquot. Then he turned to Glenn, reached his hand across the table to take the younger man's in his horseman's grip, and said, "If you're asking for my blessings, my boy, you've had them from the day we met. And if you want my opinion, Betsy will come around just as long as she knows it's her choice. She's still carrying a torch for The Duke, of course. Who wouldn't? I loved that Jewish gentleman myself, even though he was just a little too good a businessman for me and we got a bit crosswise over a deal a year or two before he disappeared. But as a husband and a father, you couldn't ask for more, even as a close friend, before our little tiff over not much money; he was aces.

"What he couldn't ever be was the son I never had. And you're just that. It's as if I had a dream about that son and woke up to find you standing in front of me, shaking my hand, every inch of you exactly what I dreamed about."

The waiter stood by holding the wine with a big DCC monogrammed napkin wrapped around it, then at Barney's signal, poured enough champagne to cover the bottom eighth of the flute and handed it to Barney to taste. Barney swirled it, sniffed the bouquet, took a sip, and pronounced it perfect, and the waiter filled both of their glasses.

Glenn, raising his glass, said, "To the loveliest lady in Texas."

"And the best catch in town," Barney topped him. Then, before Glenn could react to the possible aspersion, he added "although that's what I hear the opinion makers around here are calling you."

"If you're on side, Barney," Glenn said, "I plan to propose to both of them right away."

"Both of them?"

"Both of them. I don't stand a chance with Betsy if Dorothea isn't happy about my being her adoptive father, or stepfather, at the minimum."

"Don't you think you might want to leave that mission to Betsy?"

"If she wants me to, I will, but I'd rather do it myself."

The waiter had refilled the champagne glasses, and Barney raised his again. "Mazel tov, right?"

"Perfect," Glenn said as they clicked glasses and emptied them in one. "The Duke taught you well."

"Maybe I've got a little of the blood, along with my eighth Cherokee. Who knows? They say my grandfather was quite a ladies' man, and it was catch-as-catch can out here when he rode in."

Glenn indicated the glasses to the waiter watching from a few feet away. He filled them with the last of the wine, and they both raised and clicked their glasses again. "Nothing like a little hybrid vigor, eh, 'Dad'?" he grinned.

"Improves the breed, I say."

"That's it then, Barney, evermore." And they both knocked down the champagne, stood, shook hands, slapped each other's backs, and walked out happy.

Glenn and Betsy met that evening at one of the steak houses they liked. Glenn asked if she would drink champagne with him since this was a very special night and he had asked the house to have a bottle of what had become their choice tableside when they arrived. Betsy said she would be happy to drink it and focused wide-eyed on him, signaling her interest in hearing what the occasion was, as the wine steward poured half an ounce for Glenn to taste.

He did, approved it, and the glasses were carefully filled. Then he placed a small, plush black velvet box on the tabletop at her left hand, and said, "With Barney's permission already granted, I want to tell you I love you more than anyone I've ever known or hope to know in life, and I ask you to be my adored wife for now and forever. Will you marry me, my darling?"

"I love you more than I ever thought I could love again, my sweet, darling, dashing Glenn. And with two qualifications, I may be literally dying to accept your proposal, because if my heart were beating any faster, I might take my last ecstatic breath right here and now."

Eyes suddenly narrowing with concern, Glenn asked very softly, leaning toward her,

". . . and the qualifications?"

"Number one is crucial, but not likely to be much of a challenge for you if you handle it with your usual delicacy. You have to be seen to treat it as absolutely essential. It might sound like too much responsibility to give a child, but if we want to make this a success, we really do need Dorothea's approval."

"A given," Glenn said solemnly. "Now what's the second?"

"Not quite so easy to talk about, here and now."

"May I presume to guess?"

"If you can do that discretely, under the immediate circumstances."

"Let me try. But first, let's drink to love."

He raised his glass, she hers, they clicked and drank. Then he folded his hands on the edge of the table and gathered himself. "You had a great marriage with an unusual and apparently terrific guy. I believe he was your first and only lover. And he knew how to treat a woman, setting the pattern for what any reasonable woman would describe as a very good, loving, maybe exciting, certainly mutually satisfying love life. If he'd lived, I don't think you'd have ever considered being intimate with another man.

"We've been very careful and controlled. We haven't even come close to real intimacy. We're attracted to each other. I'm certainly head over heels in love with you. You've even developed some real affection for me, although it's still a long way from what you've known with Duke, I'm sure. And for two adults, each with some happy experience in intimacy, it's a little a bit of gamble, as you see it, to consider sharing a marital bed with somebody who may not be able to give you the kind of deeply satisfying physical relationship you've had before. And, of course, you're kind of stuck with him if the other important people in your life like him and you can see he's trying his best to please you in everything."

"Oh, Dr. Benziger, you do have some bedside manner, and you are one very insightful fellow."

Their glasses had been refilled, without their noticing, by the nearly invisible waiter. She lifted hers, touched it to his, then drained it in one long swallow.

"Doctor," she said, " your patient, or should I say, the object of your intentions, has a very good suggestion to make about satisfying what you have so gracefully avoided characterizing as her well justified curiosity and clarifying some basic facts."

She removed the velvet box from the table and disposed it somewhere on her person, then reached back across the table to grasp his still folded hands. "My suggestion is that when we have finished what I'm sure will be a lovely, and memorable dinner, we retire to your suite at the Adolphus and conduct the kind of scientific investigation that will answer the questions we have now identified."

"What a noble dedication to the pursuit of knowledge you display, my darling." The glasses had again been filled. He lifted his, she hers, and they clicked.

"To knowledge," she said.

"In the biblical sense," he responded.

"And the carnal," she added, with a glint in her eyes.

Glenn signaled for the captain.

*   *   *

Betsy slipped out of Glenn's bed before first light the next morning to dress and drive home before Dorothea awoke. Fully groomed, ready for her usual full day, she bent over the deep-sleeping Glenn's face and gently kissed his lips. He was instantly awake, turning to reach for her. She allowed him to take her left hand as she leaned away to turn on the bedside lamp just long enough for him to be able to see the large, emerald-cut diamond on her ring finger.

Then she switched off the light and whispered in his ear, "The experiment was a smashing success, Doctor Benziger. I think we've opened up a new area of behavioral science that's certain to become a major field of study. I suggest we go right back to work tonight to see if we can replicate our results."

And so they did, working avidly through much of the night, sending Betsy to her office the next morning weak-kneed and reducing Glenn to cancelling his noon squash match at the DAC.

Later that day, she placed a call to her attorney and asked him to repeat what he had told her several years before about the seven-year "rule" in law. This time she paid close attention. When they met at Betsy's home that evening, they were too busy playing with Dorothea to broach the subject uppermost in both of their minds, and without any need to agree on the plan, they both steered well clear of that subject until the child was asleep, under her nanny's watchful eye, and the two lovers settled at a table in another one of their favorite restaurants.

Over drinks, she asked him if he was familiar with the seven-year tradition, and he assured her he was, having had himself brought up to speed on it within the past few days. They had each concluded that it would be prudent to get a judge's imprimatur, and they quickly settled on Barney's old college roommate who now presided over the state's highest court. Then they rolled on into the wedding arrangements and agreed almost as quickly on a simple "family and close friends" ceremony at the county clerk's office and a big party at the country club that evening, finessing the religious choice which they felt they could think about a little longer.

Betsy assured him, *sua sponte,* that if his family had strong feelings on the subject, neither she nor Barney would have any objection to the wedding being performed at Temple Emanuel synagogue in town, where the president was a longtime investor with Barney. She and her father were raised Episcopalian, but not very rigorously so, and the marriage with Max had been notably civil, in both senses of the word. Its very evident success had tamped down most potential concerns about Betsy's marrying outside the church again, with another Semite, to boot. Even the die-hard good old boys hesitated to voice much objection in the fall of 1946 to a handsome, rich war hero just back from saving the world for democracy, who seemed to be such a decent chap and whose name sounded as Lone Star as Davey Crockett, whatever it might have been in the old country.

MAX '46 I

THEY HAD THOUGHT THROUGH JUST ABOUT EVERYTHING. THEN Betsy received a call at her office, referred by the nanny who doubled as manager of the household, a call that, until a month before, she had awaited with indefatigable hope every day for more than seven years. It came from an army captain who identified himself as John Ralston, on temporary duty at SHAEF headquarters in Vienna, and it was about a male who looked to be in his late sixties, but claimed to be just forty-five, who, with absolutely no identifying documents, insisted that he was a naturalized American citizen, somehow captured by an Iron Cross unit in Moldavia in 1939, turned over to the OGPU as a suspected spy, tortured and imprisoned there for some time before being shipped to a work camp in the Siberian Arctic, where he survived six years of hard labor and brutalization in a salt mine before managing to escape, tramp on foot across seventeen hundred miles of frozen tundra and pine forests, somehow living off the land in an area in which nothing edible was believed to have grown since the German invasion, finally stumbling into a DP camp just inside the Austrian border, and collapsing in delirium, more dead than alive, three days before. The officer's voice wavered in and out over the fragile telephone connection, but Betsy didn't miss a word.

"That's my husband, Captain," Betsy said with certainty. "His name is Max Landers."

"That's just what this fellow says, ma'am. But how did you know?"

"Because what you just described would have been impossible for anyone in the world except my husband. That man is my husband,

136

Max Landers, and I'm absolutely positive of it. I've been waiting to hear his voice for more than seven years."

"How old is your husband, Mrs . . . ."

"Forty-five, just as he says. But after what you tell me he's been through he could look a hundred. So, please, please, let's not argue over it. Just tell me how to bring him home. Can I come and get him?"

"Well, ma'am, that would be a bit difficult but if he's who you say he is and he says he is, we'll get him back to you. We'll deliver him right to your door, after we get him into better shape. But please understand I have to check this out more thoroughly. He could just be some refugee or deserter who came across enough information on your husband to try to impersonate him and use that to get into the States without waiting his turn."

"If you'll excuse me, Captain, that is my husband, damn it. And I'll be on your doorstep tomorrow morning with everything I need to prove that, if you'll go right ahead and tell me where to find you. I will nurse him back to health a lot faster and a lot better here than any army hospital can, I promise you that."

"He's not exactly in a U.S. Army hospital, ma'am. If he's who you say he is, I wish he was. He gets some treatment in a dispensary in the DP camp, and he's in a kind of dormitory, but he's not exactly living high on the hog. We haven't even established that he's a citizen. I kind of liked him right away, and I'm trying to help. That's why I'm calling you. But we've got a ways to go before he's sleeping in his own bed, even if he is who you think he is. It's complicated."

"Captain Ralston," she said, "if you were to give me a number where I can have a sitting United States senator call you, could you put my husband on the phone with him today?"

"Ma'am, if a real United States senator wants to speak to somebody around here, he's going to speak to him for sure. But why do you want to do that?"

"Because the senator, Senator Jason C. Dawes, is going to ask my husband two or three questions to be sure it's his dear friend Max Landers, and then do whatever it takes to get him on the next plane to Dallas."

"Ma'am, United States senators get whatever they want around here, without too many questions asked, but, with respect, could I just say something personal to you before you go setting that up?"

"If you're going to help get my husband back home as soon as possible, you can say anything an officer and a gentleman would say to a lady, and I'll thank you for it, Captain."

"Well, ma'am, this man we have here has been very, very roughed up. He's only alive because he's tough as old shoe leather and unbelievably determined. But he is a sight to scare someone who loves him, and if that Senator Dawes could get him into a good hospital here, or even the base infirmary for a little while so he's feeling better and looks more like he's gonna make it, his homecoming would go a lot better for him and for you. Do you understand what I am trying to tell you? He's been through holy hell, ma'am, and he shows it."

"Captain, you're a good man. I can tell that. And I appreciate it. But if I lost my Max all over again, now . . . and I think you're trying to tell me I could, it's that bad, I couldn't take it. Not again. So I must have him here, where I can take care of him, just as fast as possible. Can you understand me?"

"Yes, ma'am, I sure can," he said, "and I'm beginning to think old Max might just be a whole lot luckier man than I realized he was." He gave her the number of the telephone he could answer and told her he'd stand by it until he heard from the senator. Two hours later, the call came in from Dawes and after paying his respects to the senator, the captain said Mr. Landers was sitting at the same desk, wide awake after napping from the minute he sat down until the phone rang, with brief interruptions every time it had rung for calls on matters not concerning him.

Dawes asked the captain to put Max on the line.

Max said, "How are you, Jase? It's been a long time, hasn't it?"

"It sure as hell has, Max. How are you? You don't sound so good. Is that really you?" Max's rough foreign accent didn't make him sound like the King's English speaker the senator knew.

"To tell you the truth, Jase, I could be a little better. Thanks for asking. But I'm alive and almost kicking. That's the good part. The rest I'll fill in when I see you. But how are Betsy and my daughter and Barney? They must have set up this call. Tell me how they are."

"They're just fine, now that they know you're alive. But I won't waste a minute getting you home, my friend. So just tell me, what color suits do I wear?"

"How am I going to forget that? Only one: Cambridge gray, in any weight, in any pattern, just Cambridge gray, except in a dinner jacket or tails."

"Put that Ralston fellow back on the line, Max. And you take it easy on the way home, boy, you hear? You sound awful, like something the cat dragged in, only from Moscow, or wherever. But we're gonna fix you up. You better believe it."

"I know, Jase, and thanks. Take care of yourself. I'll see you soon. Don't worry about me." Then, to the captain, "He wants to talk to you again, Captain."

"Captain Ralston," Jason C. Dawes said in his no-mike platform voice booming over the crackling line so Max, slumping back in his chair, could hear it four feet away from the receiver pressed to Ralston's ear, "now you hear this. I want that man as comfortable as the United States Army Air Corps can make him, with a full-fledged real doctor by his side, and a nurse, taking turns watching him every minute of the way, on the first transport plane you can get your hands on to fly him back to Dallas, Texas, and an ambulance, not a Jeep, mind you, a regular ambulance, meeting that plane and taking him straight to Methodist Hospital where that doctor is going to check him in, explain what's wrong with him to the right specialists, and see that he's properly settled before the sun sets tomorrow, you hear? And you tell that doctor who comes with him to tell those doctors at Methodist that I will be calling them tomorrow night, for a full report. You hear, son? You got all that?"

"Yes, Senator," said the captain. "I've got it all, and we'll send along everything we have on him, medical and otherwise, although it isn't much, sir."

"Well, I do thank you, Captain, for giving this matter your full attention," he continued in a more conversational tone. "I can see you recognize the importance of this mission. And I'd like to make one more suggestion. You tell your CO I said if you can be spared from what I am sure are your other vital duties for this brief period, I want you to fly right along with Mr. Landers and the doctor and the nurse on this mission just to be sure there's no snafu on the Dallas end, and you keep me posted through my Washington office starting as soon as you land tomorrow, if not sooner. And you can also tell your CO I'd like him to authorize the whole crew, flight, medical, and yourself, to take a week visiting your own homes before you fly back to base.

"I thank you again, Captain," and he rang off.

Max was in bed in his hospital suite, hooked up to an IV, and under round-the-clock surveillance, in Dallas Methodist Hospital, before 7:00 p.m. Central Time the following day. Betsy and Barney were resting in armchairs, a few feet away in the sitting room of the suite while he slept. They, too, were recovering from what they'd seen as he was wheeled in.

"I'm wondering whom to tell first," she said.

"I think it's a clear call, Bets. You have to level with Glenn right away, or at least as soon as you've decided what to do. I think you've got a little time before you have to tell Max everything. At least until you've had a chance to see what his chances of recovery are. Hearing the news might really put him away."

"You think you know Max, Dad. I know I do. He'll survive. I'm not even surprised he lived through those years in the salt mines, no matter how tough they were, or that he escaped and reached Austria alive. There's nobody like him. He's indomitable, Dad. I'm not saying he'll never die. But I really believe that will only happen when he wants it to."

"When he learns the situation, he might want to check out. He's a wreck, beyond repair is my guess. What kind of life would he have after all this, and without you and Dorothea?"

"It doesn't have to be that way, Dad."

"You mean you'd pick up your life with him, just as if nothing happened? As if he hadn't decided, all on his own to run off halfway around the world, leaving his wife and child behind, to try and save some doomed people he didn't even know. It's not as if he was drafted. He just decided on his own he had to go. Or he wanted to go. And he disappeared, for seven years.

"Aren't you in love with Glenn? Are you just going to tell him, 'Sorry, The Duke isn't dead. You'll have to pack up and go back to Chicago, find somebody else to fall in love with'?"

"It's certainly not that simple, Dad. I just have to think it all through, and I'm not ready to do that right this minute."

"Well, of course you have to think about it. I certainly hope you do, and if you need time, I understand that. Take time, and think it through carefully. It's probably the biggest decision you'll ever make in your life. But I don't think you want to keep Glenn in the dark any longer than you absolutely have to. He ought to know what's going on, and know it from you, unless you want me to tell him."

"No, Dad. That's my job. But I've got to think it through before I do. Isn't the first thing Glenn will ask me, what does all this mean to us? And how do I answer that now, when I don't really know yet, myself?"

"You do know Max can't ever be what he was, even if he survives."

"I don't even know that, Dad."

"I do. If he makes it, he'll be an old man."

"Dad, stop. Please stop. You don't know Max as I do. Maybe you don't even know me as well as you think."

"I know both of you well enough to know you can't put Humpty Dumpty together again. And I know Glenn is a once-in-a lifetime guy. I'd put my money on that . . ."

"Dad, stop. Please just stop now."

"OK. I've stopped."

"We'll discuss it again, when I can, I promise you."

"OK."

*　　*　　*

The efforts Max had been able to make to bring himself to the attention of Captain Ralston and convince him to call Betsy, then later to talk over the telephone with Senator Dawes, were astonishing, spasmodic expressions of his will to survive, overcoming his utter physical and mental devastation. He had not been fully conscious since the exchange with Dawes. He sank back into alternating states of unconsciousness and delirium, virtually incapable of conscious speech or thought. The doctor who had been at his side throughout the flight from Vienna concluded and noted that Max was suffering from typhus, probably pleurisy or walking pneumonia, consequences of severe dehydration, hypothermia, and profound exhaustion, a raging infection in his right foot, presumably from a suppurating wound on the sole, another of unknown cause in his left eye, cuts, bruises, scrapes on much of his exposed epidermis, his tongue and the inner surfaces of his mouth and ears, the bridge of nose, his scalp and hands, and his teeth were worn down to sharpened stubs.

While Betsy and Barney were talking in the sitting room, they could hear him coughing violently in his sleep, and at one moment, both rushed into his room in response to the scream of a nurse who reported that when she had tried to adjust the sheet covering his body up to the chest, he had, momentarily waking, or possibly still unconscious, gripped both her arms with enough force to bruise the skin and from his supine position hurled her across the room and against a wall, shouting "Nyet, nyet!" in fury. She was led away to recover and replaced by two big male nurses.

The army doctors' rough diagnosis had been confirmed by hospital staff, and a medication regime through the IV was initiated, along with sedation carefully introduced to avoid aggravation of his breathing problems or bring on any interference with his steady heart function, despite an unusually low pulse rate. The senior resident coordinating Max's care explained that the special quarters established for the patient in a very crowded urban hospital/medical center reflected two factors of significance: the senator's insistence on "the best," with the cost "no issue," and the necessity to seal off the rest of the hospital, to the greatest degree possible, from the potential contagion threat presented by the patient's assortment of infections and diseases. The resident also reassured her that although Max had enough wrong with him to bring most men to death's door and was, by any standard, a very sick man, his vital signs indicated that he was not in grave danger.

Betsy, sensing the young doctor who had mentioned his military service to her, had enough confidence to answer straightforwardly, asked him directly, "Do you think he's going to make it?"

He winked. "I've seen a lot worse make it in much less competent facilities when I was an army doctor. And your man, if that's what he is, is one tough guy, ma'am. It's gonna take a while, but my money's on him. He'll make it."

After thanking him warmly for the encouragement, without the slightest trace of flirtation, Betsy hesitated for a moment, checked her watch, and then asked the doctor if he thought Max would sleep through the night.

"Ma'am," he said, "if there's any way he knows you're right here waiting for him, there's no telling what he might do, but on strictly medical grounds, sick as he is, exhausted as he is, and with as much medication as he has in him, I'd say he's more likely to sleep another thirty or forty hours, passively glucosed and hydrated through that IV and relieved through his catheter. You can safely go home and get some rest yourself, which, if you'll forgive me, you look as if you could use right now. He'll be all right with us."

"Can we get private nurse coverage full time?"

"I'm not sure it's necessary, round the clock, but there is an RN sitting right outside the door of his suite, listening very carefully. And the order says 'whatever he needs' so he can have it if you want it. I'll get the head of the service on it when I pass her station. And I'll be stopping by on my rounds, just checking. G'won home, ma'am. Get some rest. You're gonna need it for the long haul."

"More than you know, Doctor. More than you'll ever know."

"That's Gershwin, ma'am. Great tune. I used to play a little tenor sax, very little, and sing worse. But that song made even me sound pretty good."

"I'll bet you did, Doctor. I'll thank you again and say good night."

"You're most welcome, ma'am. It's my pleasure."

"Take good care of that man, please. To say it in Gershwin, too, it's '. . . my man, I love him so.' He's been gone so long I'd forgotten how much."

She touched the doctor's forearm gently, waved good night, and started home. She had driven herself to the hospital, and then put in a fourteen-hour stint in the suite without making any special effort to think through her bizarre position. And she knew she was much too fatigued to risk trying to parse it out while struggling to focus on the road. As she reached the driveway to the home she had designed for herself and Max, she was hoping to slip in quietly, bathe, fix herself a scotch, stretch out on her chaise longue, and begin her customary process of breaking down complex problems with a conscious review before she fell asleep, an unconscious analysis while she slept, and a clear decision taking shape over her morning coffee.

But the timing didn't work. She saw Glenn's convertible parked outside the garage and knew the long night had just begun. He opened the front door for her and took her in his arms, crushing her to him, pressing his lips to her neck for a long moment until he said, "My poor darling, what must be whirling through your mind. But I want you to know, we'll deal with whatever we have to and handle everything in the best possible way for you and Dorothea. That's all I care about. What's best for the two of you." And he led her gently into the library and onto a leather lounge chair and ottoman. He spread a light throw over her body and moved to the drinks table where he poured two scotches over ice in old-fashioned glasses, brought her one, kept the other, and sat down in the facing chair.

"I can just imagine, my love. At least the confusion and the riot of emotions. What you're going to do, I can't imagine. All I know is that I love you more than anything in life, and whatever is right for you and Dorothy, I will do everything in my power to make happen, as easily and as gracefully as possible."

"I know you will, Glenn. That's one of the reasons why I love you so. For all of your star quality, you really are the most decent of men. The unbelievable irony is that Max is cut from the same cloth. You are, incredibly, the two best men I've ever known. Completely different backgrounds. But the same men, to a tee. The best of breed. How could anybody even dream of this happening to the three of us? Not that I'm in the same league with either of you. I'm not disparaging myself. I have my virtues, but you two are, what can I say, just head and shoulders—"

"Betsy, you're a fabulous woman. I'm just a decent guy from a prominent family who happened to have a good war and, aside from that, all I really know about what I want to do with my life is that I want to spend it with you, and thanks to my family's money, I can give you and Dorothea a good life. How you happened to fall in love with me, I don't really understand. I'm just a work in progress. But from what I understand about 'Duke,' he's the real American hero. The self-made supersuccess everybody admires and almost everybody likes a helluva lot. And until about a month ago, he was your husband. He's the real thing. I'm not anything yet."

Betsy held her drink in both hands and smiled over the rim at him. "Don't try to tell that to any nubile woman in Chicago or Dallas, darling. You're the catch of the decade, and everybody knows it. Max may have been The Duke of Dallas before he left, but you, by all reports—and I've heard them in detail—were and still are the Prince of Chicago."

"Do you think Max and I are going to have to have to duel for your hand?"

"Maybe we can all live together," she said, with an ironic smile.

Glenn ran his index figure over the rim of his glass. Then he said very seriously, "That depends, I guess, on how old he feels he is."

"I know. Max is a very hard-eyed realist. Big heart, very loving, and believes almost everything is possible if you want it enough. But he never kids himself. And he calculates odds automatically on anything. He may not know how much of what he was he can be again right now, but once he can think straight, he'll know. He doesn't confuse hopes and illusions. You'll see."

"So let me suggest this, my darling. Why don't we give The Duke a little time to mend and take stock, and then have this discussion three ways, when he's up to it?" Then he stood and put his glass back on the drinks table. "And for right now, why don't you go up and give Dorothea a kiss and get some sleep for yourself. I'll head back to my place and hope for the best."

"I'd get a better night's sleep in your arms."

"Not here you wouldn't. And I don't think that would be playing quite fair right now. Let's take a little time and give Max some, too. OK, darling?"

"Marquis of Queensbury, eh?"

"Nothing less. Noblesse oblige."

"Good night, sweet prince."

DANNY '89

PETER'S ASSISTANT CALLED HIM IN THE MAIN CONFERENCE ROOM shortly after ten a.m. and said that she had a Phillip Moynihan on the line insisting on speaking to him. Peter apologized to the group around the table, drew the coiled cord out as far toward the door as it would stretch, and greeted his former justice department colleague formally. "Yessir, how can I help you?"

"That depends on how well you're playing," Moynihan answered.

"I've got a murderous schedule, sir," Peter answered, with as little hint of camaraderie as possible.

"I would, too, billing at $400 an hour," said the deputy U.S. attorney for the Southern District. "But frankly, I've been working my ass off in the public interest for the past month, and I could use a day at boys' camp."

"What day did you have in mind, sir?"

"Tomorrow," said the federal prosecutor.

"And what were you planning, sir?" Peter asked.

"I pick you up at 8:30. Tennis at Travis Island in the morning, say nine. Then lunch and golf at your place right afterward. Does that schedule work for you, Counselor?"

"Absolutely, sir, 8:30 a.m. it is. I'll be on time."

"Very good, Counselor. I'm looking forward to your cooperation."

"Well, we'll have to discuss that."

"Be prepared to give me your full attention."

"You can count on that, sir."

They both rang off.

147

Moynihan had played number 1 for Fordham Prep for both his junior and senior years, then moved up from 4 to 3 to 2 to 1 at BC. Neither of them could remember who was ahead in their personal mano a mano, but they both knew it was razorblade close. They also knew that neither one had yet become a seriously competitive golfer, but any game, anywhere, they'd play out to the last stroke as though their lives depended on it. And they loved every minute of the battle.

They let lunch go at Quaker Ridge and rushed through hot dogs at the turn before finally sitting down over drinks at the bar in the middle of the afternoon, still juiced on the competition.

"You never change," Peter said. "Every call goes your way."

"How many bad calls did I make on the golf course?" Moynihan asked.

"If there'd been any to make, you'd have made them," Peter said.

Then Phil turned suddenly serious. "Your old buddy, Danny Boy, is number one on the hit parade. Are you aware of that?"

"Frankly, no," Peter said. "Although I can't say I'm exactly stunned, Phil. He's a nasty SOB and a real bad boy."

"We know all that. But we didn't know you did. You want to help us nail him?"

"I don't think I can. Most of what I know, I can't give you. But let me think it through before I say no. I'd love to see you put him away. He's no damned good. Slick as a wharf rat, but maybe, just maybe not as smart as he thinks he is. Give me a few days. I've got real ethics problems, and I have to be careful."

"We know he's been in your office more than once. And Peter, whatever he offers you, don't take it. He's dead, and if you represent him, you could get hurt, too."

"Don't worry about that."

"I do, Peter. You're one of us, and I don't want to see you taken down with him. So you worry about it, too. Don't let that menace get his hooks into you. You hear me?"

"I hear you."

"You were very close once. Does he have anything on you?"

"I despise him."

"Peter, that may not be enough. You have to fear him, too. He's that bad, and he's that smart, believe me. The only way I'd be sure you were all right is if you were working with us to nail him."

"I've got to think about it. Let me do that."

"Peter, you've got much more to worry about from the U.S. Attorney than the Bar Association. Find a way. I don't want to see you befouled by that creep."

"Phil, I appreciate it. I know what you mean. We learned the ropes together. And if I were in your position, with you in mine, I'd be trying to protect your ass, too. Believe me, I understand. But let me think."

"Sure, Pete, think all you want. Just come up with the right answer."

They drove back from Quaker to the city in Phil's car, talking about everything but the central issue between them at the moment.

MAX '46 II

BETSY WALKED TO THE FRONT DOOR WITH GLENN. THEY KISSED, held each other for a moment, then pressed their cheeks together as Glenn whispered in her ear, "I'm going to do everything I can to see that we don't lose what we have, my love."

"Thank you, darling. I need to know we'll work our way through this together. Right now, I'm too exhausted to think straight, and I haven't even explained what's happened to Dorothea. And I must before she hears about it from somebody else. That's my first concern. I'm hoping I wake up in the morning with some idea of what this is all going to mean before I try to explain it to her."

"I don't think it's going to be that easy, love. But if we're together, we can handle whatever comes at us, and that's my plan. When you do wake up tomorrow, I hope that's your plan, too. Now, try to get some sleep."

"I hope I will. I'm staggering. But before you go, please tell me how you heard about this so fast. I'm bewildered."

"How did I know Max was back?"

"Yes. I'm not sure he even knows where he is."

"Darling, everybody in town knows Max Landers is back. And they assume he's expecting to pick up right where he left off seven years ago, with his wife and child, his home, his businesses, his friends, and his fortune. And since it's pretty widely known that our wedding is scheduled for a week from Saturday, there's a lot of speculation on how this is all going to end up. But you try to get some rest now, before you do any more heavy thinking. Just know I'm right here with you, every step. You can count on that, no matter

150

what happens." He hugged her, brushed his lips over hers, and headed out to his car as she closed the door behind him.

Barney was their first visitor in the morning. He knew Dorothea was awakened by her nanny at 7:00, and he had made it his business to be there half an hour before.

The nanny tapped lightly on Betsy's bedroom door, then slipped in, crossed the room to rouse her gently, and waited for her eyes to open and focus. "Your father is here, Mrs. Landers. He thought it would be a good idea if he took Dorothea to his place this morning and called the school to say she'd be getting there a little late. I think that's a good idea, too, unless you already know just what you want to tell her and you're ready to answer some complicated questions."

Betsy stretched, reached for a dressing gown across the foot of her bed, and slipped her arms into it before throwing her legs out from under the covers and closing the gown as she stood.

"OK," she said, "but I'd like to talk to him before he sees her. Please tell him I'll be down in five minutes."

"He's waiting in the breakfast room. I'll tell him you'll be right down. But are you all right? Is there anything I can do for you?"

"Thanks, Martha," Betsy answered, appreciatively. "I'm a little shaky, but I'll get myself together. We'll talk after my dad and Dorothea leave. And I do want to see her before they go, so please be sure they save a couple of minutes for me, just long enough for me to tell her I love her and that we'll have a good talk when I pick her up this afternoon. Please do not discuss my husband."

"Yes, ma'am. Just as you say."

"Thank you. And please don't worry yourself. Everything is going to be worked out in Dorothea's best interests. There's not going to be turmoil. You have my word on it."

The nanny nodded and left for the breakfast room. Betsy was there a few minutes later, still in her dressing gown, teeth brushed, hair brushed, best smile. She kissed her father on the forehead, and he pulled her to him, head on her shoulder.

"Oh, kiddo," he said softly, muffled, a catch in his throat. "You've really got your hands full. I slept about two hours and thought hard the rest of the night. But I didn't come close to a good idea."

"Neither did I," Betsy said, pulling away, taking the chair to his left.

The houseman/driver entered quietly with juice, fruit, and coffee for her. He'd already served Barney.

"Good morning, ma'am," he said, as he slipped the plates quietly in front of her and poured her coffee. She greeted him and thanked him.

Lifting her cup and holding it just in front of her chin with both hands, Betsy answered her father. "Let me correct that, Dad. I don't know how right it is, but I did have a thought. Maybe a hope is a better way to say it."

"I can use one, at this point. Let's hear it."

"Well," she began, "the Max I knew was flat-out the best man I ever came across, Dad. In some ways, even better than you, and you're a very hard man to beat."

"He was better, Betsy. I had a running start. He came from nowhere—way, way, *way* behind the eight ball. And he did everything a man can do. Some of it he wouldn't be so proud to tell you about. But he did what he had to. And once he was past having to be so tough, he became the finest gentleman you'd ever want to meet. Fair to a fault, honest as the day was long, ready to give anybody a break. You could trust him with your money, your wife, your life. Or your only child, as I did, without a minute's hesitation. If you had a problem, he made it his. If you lost your temper, he'd kid you out of it, remind you that you were better than that . . ."

"Didn't you once have a business problem with him?"

"Yes, I did. And I was wrong. And I never made that mistake with him again. You never ask Max to break a commitment. That's one thing he won't do for anybody. So forget that. He was right, and I was wrong. Take it from me. I never met a straighter man. I never met a better man."

She picked at the fruit with her fork. "That's what I remember, too, Dad. Best of breed. Even the worst bigots admired him. The ones who shunned him ended up on his team. And he forgave most of them. He usually said they didn't know any better."

"That's not going to make things any easier."

"I'm not so sure of that," she said. "Remember, Dad, you always said he was much more than brilliant. He was actually wise."

"I never said he was a saint, if that's what you're counting on."

"I'm not counting on anything. I'm just saying he was a remarkable man, and his empathy was one of the things that made him so special. Of course, after what I understand he went through these past seven years, he could be wholly different now and probably is."

"How is Glenn taking this?"

"Like a man, as you'd expect. But he knows what he wants. And there's not enough to go round."

Then, in a light, musical voice, Dorothea was calling out to her nanny, "I'll be right back, I promise," and bounding into the breakfast room in her pajamas, first to throw her arms around Betsy, and then to plant a kiss on Barney's cheek, then back to hug Betsy again. "I was worried about you, Mommy. You always call if you can't make it home before I go to bed."

"You're absolutely right, and I owe you an apology, darling. But I'll be here waiting for you when you get home this afternoon, and I'll explain everything, I promise. Will you forgive me this once?"

"I'll forgive you, but I want all the details later. Now I've got to run and get ready for Grandpa to take me to school. That's a real treat." She kissed them both and hurried back to her suite.

"Have you decided what to tell her?" Barney asked.

"Not yet."

"So I say nothing?"

"At least this morning."

"And then?"

"I'd like to see what happens today."

"It doesn't sound as if you'll know any more tonight than you know now."

"Maybe not. I still need to get through the day before I make any decisions, though."

"It's your call. But I'm available to you anytime. I'll leave word to put you through immediately if you call. And I mean *anytime*. If I'm out, they'll know where to reach me. You have to let me give you a hand on this. You know I have great faith in your judgment. You're as sound as anyone. But this is so exceptional; it's the kind of problem no one's got any precedent for, so you need to talk it through with someone reasonably objective who knows the whole story. I'm your man, for all the reasons you know very well. Please, use me."

"Dad, I promise you I will. But try to calm down. Your blood pressure is going through the roof. I can see it. I do need you, very much, particularly right now. But I'd really be grateful if as soon as you drop Dorothea off at school, you'd drive over to Dr. Layton's office and have your pressure checked. And if it's elevated, get some medication to bring it down. He'll always squeeze you in if you go right over. And please, use my driver if your man isn't with you this morning."

"My driver's here. So I'll go in and get Dorothea and start on my rounds. I'll check with you here or at the hospital to tell you I'm all right and you can stop worrying about that. I don't feel as if my pressure's up. And I can usually tell. Sure I'm worried, but I know you'll work this out. I just want to help. That's the strain you see in my face, not my hypertension." He stood, leaned over to kiss her forehead, and walked off to collect his granddaughter, while Betsy sat over her coffee thinking.

An hour later, she was at the hospital trying to get a more detailed report than they would give her over the phone. The resident told her Max had slept intermittently, awakened agitated several times during the night, kept talking in his sleep, in languages no attendant understood except for the tone, which was clearly belligerent. One orderly, trying to pacify him, got too close to Max and was yanked across the bed to whack his head against the window and crack the glass in place. The resident said Max was under full-time surveillance, the equivalent of a suicide watch, but the doctor did not see any deterioration in his vital signs or attribute his prolonged sleep to anything more morbid than extreme exhaustion.

While they were talking a few feet from his bedside, Max, in a roughened version of his old, familiar voice, said, "Where am I?" in English.

Momentarily startled, Betsy rushed to his side and the doctor, more calmly, stepped up beside her.

"You're home, darling, at least, almost home. You're in the hospital, here at Dallas Methodist, recovering from your ordeal. But you are home and on the mend."

"Don't I get a welcome home kiss?"

Betsy leaned to him and kissed him on the lips, holding his battered, emaciated face between her hands. He tried to move his arms to embrace her and realized, for the first time, that his right arm was loosely tied to the bed frame, his left moored to the IV apparatus.

"My memory's a little fuzzy," Max said. "But can someone tell me how I got here and when, and why I'm tied down?"

The doctor stepped in at that. "We'll answer all your questions as well as we can. But first let me loosen the restraints and check you out for a few minutes to be sure you can handle it." While he spoke, the doctor untied the slipknot holding Max's right arm restraint in place.

"Handle what?" he said. "I'm OK. Just a little woozy."

"That may very well be, Mr. Landers, but if it's true, you've made one of the most remarkable recoveries I've ever seen. So let's try to confirm that." And stethoscope in hand, the doctor began his process while Betsy, saying she would be right outside, stepped into the sitting room to wait.

Less than fifteen minutes later, the doctor knocked lightly on the outside door of the sitting room and entered quietly to take a chair next to hers. Then he leaned towards her, with his hands folded on his knee and said: "He's in surprisingly good shape for what I understand he's been through. I'd say amazing shape, despite some substantial loss of body mass and moderately impaired lung function. Of course, it will take a little while for the tests to come back, and we can be much more definitive when we have them. But I don't think he's in serious, physical danger. I'm not qualified to evaluate his mental state, but on the basis of my interaction with him this morning, I would say he appears rational and functional.

"That incident last night might have been a bad dream or a habituated defensive reflex that developed during his incarceration. There's no sign of hostility this morning. He's charming and, incredibly, actually very funny, in a wry kind of way.

"But I want to confirm something. When you provided his personal information to the admissions people, you said he was born in 1905. Is that right?"

"I believe so. In fact, I'm pretty sure of it."

"Well, one of the consequences of what he's endured the last few years, at least, is that today, he's a good deal older than a man forty-five should be. Physically, although he appears so far to be remarkably strong, he's a man of around sixty-five, maybe even older. Again, that's physically. Whatever he's been through has made him age prematurely, at least twenty years more than the chronology suggests. And if that's true physically, the concomitant mental and emotional damage could be at least as severe. So whatever you tell him, be mindful of that. I couldn't guess what resiliency he has left, and I would try to avoid challenging it too much."

Betsy took that in and thanked the resident for his concern. Then she asked when she could go back into Max's room.

"I'll ask the nurses to let you know as soon as it's appropriate. And good luck to both of you. I'll be around until early evening. Call me if you need me."

When he'd left the suite, Betsy sat back and began to review what she had to tell her former husband and how to tell it. She'd been working the problem through, awake and asleep, ever since she learned that he, or someone claiming to be Max Landers, had turned up at the DP camp in Austria. And she had concluded, assuming he did not already know the sequence of events which had led to the present dilemma, there were two different possible approaches to giving him the facts, for each of which she could make a case, but neither of them, again assuming he did not already understand the facts, eliminated the risk of shocking him, exactly what she'd been warned about. She would have liked to avoid taking that risk, but the circumstances appeared to deny her the option.

She could approach the revelations from the perspective of the legal implications, or she could cite the emotional effects of his disappearance on her and Dorothea. And since she had always found manipulation through guilt or sympathy offensive, she was drawn to the legal tack, because it also seemed more objective and, ironically, less confrontational. Her final review, in the hard light of a Dallas winter morning, brought her to the same conclusion.

She stood, smoothed her skirt, checked her hair and makeup in the mirror on the wall separating the two rooms, and squared her shoulders, just as a nurse opened the door between them and announced that Betsy was welcome to come back in to see her husband.

She kissed him again, this time on the forehead, as she had her father, and took the metal chair beside his bed. Then, in straightforward terms and modulated tones she explained how he had become legally dead. Her account could be heard, inevitably, as making the emotional case by implication, and she knew it. But she intentionally avoided any reference to her own pain or Dorothea's. She played strictly fair. And she knew her man. Max heard her five-minute peroration in silence, smiling wearily, but not unkindly, as she laid out the story. Only when she ended by ultimately acknowledging that giving up the hope of his return, symbolized by formally swearing to the futility of her efforts to find him, was the most difficult act of her life, did he very softly say, "Betsy, my darling, I do understand. I don't believe there was any other reasonable thing you could have done after seven years."

"Of course the financial arrangements—" she began.

But he interrupted, gently, saying, "—will remain exactly as they are. There's nothing to discuss on that score. The only thing I have to say is that I am, and always will be, inexpressibly sorry to have put you and Dorothea through what I did. That I believed I had to do it is certainly true. But I did not even properly consider what might happen and, of course, ultimately did happen and brought you so much anguish.

"Things had gone my way for so long, after a rocky start in life, that I had come to believe they always would. If I had seriously thought about the possibility that it would actually go the way it did, I would never have taken on my 'mission,' loving you as much as I did then, and do today.

"There was a French Catholic communist labor leader who somehow ended up in the mines with me. He had three degrees from the Sorbonne and felt some compulsion to improve my formal education, which he certainly did. He had a sense of humor, too. And he told me I was a Jewish Joan of Arc who would end up just as badly as she did.

"So he was right, and he was wrong, like most of us. But to you and our child, I was much more wrong than right. I did actually save some lives, but I broke the hearts of the two people in the world I loved most. I'm the one who owes you an abject apology, you and Dorothea. My judgment was hopelessly wrong."

Betsy said gently, "You've got to see her as soon as possible. You'll be a very proud father."

"Absolutely. Whenever you say. But I need to know a few things first."

"Ask away."

"Is there a man in your life now?"

"Yes."

"Does he make you happy?"

"Yes, almost as happy as we were. And that's saying a lot."

"Good. Would he make a good father to Dorothea?"

"Yes."

"Will you marry him?"

"We were supposed to be married next Saturday."

"Go ahead with the wedding."

"I think that's a little soon under the circumstances."

"Because I somehow managed to pull a Lazarus?"

"In a way, yes."

"Betsy, you're a young, vital, incredibly beautiful woman. If after all this agony, you've found a young man who can be the husband you deserve and the father Dorothea needs, which I certainly can't be, no matter how much I wish I could, please do not delay the wedding. We'll find some other role in the family for me."

"What would you have in mind?"

"A second grandfather, or a great-uncle. That's about my speed these days. I could never be what I was to you. That I've got to accept, and so do you."

"We have time to decide that when you've made a full recovery."

"No, my love. We decide that right now. I tore your life apart once. You've had the good sense to put it right. And you've obviously found the right man to do it with. If he weren't, Barney would have run him off the ranch long before now. It's a given he's a good man, the right man. You two get married now and start your new life together, and Dorothea's new life with you both, on the right foot. I'll be around to help, not compete. I want that to be absolutely clear, or I leave Dallas as soon as I can get out of this bed."

"Max—"

"No negotiation. We sign off right now."

"We were very good together, Max."

"So that's great to remember. It proved you could do it. Now you know you can do it again."

"I could with you, too."

"I wish I could say I could. I can't. You'll just have to settle for the new and improved version. And Barney will have to settle for splitting the grandpa job with me, and if that old blue blood makes a fuss, I'll straighten him out. Leave that to me."

"This is really what you want, Max?"

"It's more than I deserve. I plan to make the best of it."

"No discussion with Barney?"

"What's he got to do with our decision? It's your new husband who should get a vote. I think you'd better talk to him right away."

"Barney was here last night until he nearly fell asleep on his feet. You can bet he'll be here later today after he brings Dorothea home from school. Especially when he knows you can talk back to him."

"So send him in. And, my darling girl, put that wedding back on the tracks and get the lucky man—What's his name, by the way?—over here, too. I want to meet my son-in-law and make sure I approve."

Seven hours later, they were all in the suite, with the door between the rooms open, working their way through the second bottle of pre-Prohibition Glenfiddich from Barney's cellar, all but Dorothea, mesmerized by the new old man in her life and happily nursing her coke through the laughter and the protests of the nurses who kept returning in teams to tell them booze was strictly prohibited in the hospital. They warned everyone, but Max reassured them that if the homemade vodka in the mining barracks hadn't killed him, twenty-five-year-old single malt scotch whiskey wouldn't either.

DANNY '90 III

MOYNIHAN GAVE ME TWO DAYS TO THINK OVER HIS PROPOSITION, AND I wrestled with the ethical concerns between meetings throughout the first day. By late afternoon I wanted to bring the judge into the process because he was more familiar with the facts than anyone else in the firm and had been my guide through the ethical maze from the early going. He had also been a federal prosecutor under Bobby Kennedy and thoroughly understood what cooperating with the U.S. Attorney would entail.

We met in my office, and when I started to explain the latest twist, he acknowledged he had known it was very likely to be developing. "The prosecutor wins both ways," he said, "denying you to Miller and recruiting you for his side. But I think you have a conflict Miller will never waive."

When I agreed that was a likely scenario, Farkas reminded me of the agreement we had reached after the "incident" several months before. "Your primary obligation here is to the firm," he said. "We are talking about a major case. Probably a high seven-figure fee, maximum visibility, a bases-loaded home run. You win it, and you're on the all-star team. Lose it after a commendable defense, and you're still a big hitter. Your 'friend,' the Deputy U.S. Attorney for the Southern District is trying to con you. You do not suffer any professional damage because you defend a bad guy, win or lose, so long as you give him your best effort. It's win-win for you and for the firm. You have to take the case."

"That gives no weight at all to the fact that I know just how bad a guy Miller is and have good reason to believe he's guilty of at least some of the charges he's going to face."

161

"As I've said before, and you certainly know without my telling you, it's not our role to judge him. Guilty or not, he's entitled to the best defense we can give him."

"But not necessarily from me."

"I think you have to let the firm decide that. Let's put it to the partners."

"We both know how that'll turn out."

"Yes. I'm sure we do. But isn't that the point?"

"From the firm's perspective, I guess it is."

"We are a partnership, Peter. A partnership of lawyers. There is no other perspective that's relevant."

I sat back, tented my fingers, and thought for a moment. I knew he was right, of course, but the very idea still repelled me. I finally said, "You're convinced I really don't have a choice."

"I'm not saying that. You could resign from the firm. That is a choice you could make. It's one I wouldn't want to see you make. In fact, I'd hate to see you make it. But that is certainly a choice you could make. The wrong one, but an alternative."

"How would the partners respond to that?"

"With regret," he said. "How they'd spin it is another matter you'd have to consider."

There was really no point in stretching it out. "OK," I said. "I'll represent him, but I'm going to call Moynihan before I call Miller."

"If you think that's what best serves your client's interests, go ahead."

"At the moment, Miller is not yet my client, so before I join his team I'm going to make my peace with his adversaries, since my heart is really with them. That's one decision I can make on my own."

"I'm not so sure of that, Peter . . ."

"With respect, Judge, I am," I said. "And I'm not about to debate that issue, even with you."

I called Moynihan that afternoon and made a date to meet him for a drink at the Yale Club at the end of the day. He wasn't really surprised, but he was even angrier than I thought he'd be.

"Just tell me, Peter, wouldn't you love to nail the son-of-a-bitch?"

"What do you think?" I asked him.

"I think you've sold out," he said. "I thought you were still one of us in your gut. It sickens me."

"Then you'd better stay out of private practice," I said. "It's all about the client, no matter what kind of a scoundrel he is. Those are the rules. The Golden Rules, in fact."

"Yeah, the guy who's got the gold . . . etcetera, etcetera. I'm goddamned sick of that, too."

"You can beat him."

"Sure," he said. "All I have to do is beat you. What a crock of shit."

"Can I give you a word of advice?" I asked him.

"Sure."

"Squeeze everybody, friend or foe. Somebody will break down."

"Don't worry. I'm not going to pull any punches. You remember that Red Sox right fielder who was tearing the cover off the ball until he got hit in the eye?"

"Sure," I said. "Petrocelli. He was going to be great."

"First name?" Moynihan asked.

"Rico."

"Don't forget that."

"How many times have you heard me say it was never intended for this kind of case?"

"Miller's not a racketeer?"

"Not in the RICO sense."

"When you have a very smart, very bad guy in your sights, you use what the law gives you. We know that's exactly what he'll do with you as his lawyer."

"If the firm says I have to defend him, I will use anything I can to forestall the indictment, and if you get it, as you probably will, if only on the ham sandwich theory, I'll fight you all the way to the verdict. You're not going to have any slam dunk."

"Exactly what I'm worried about. You're a damn good criminal lawyer. And you can make this look like a victimless crime."

"But you can certainly make the case that it is a pattern of crimes involving a lot of money."

"So let's assume I get the indictment since you're not even in the room. When we go to trial, assuming he doesn't cop a plea, he's one defendant who will take the stand and charm the jury, he's that slick."

"You'll have to bury him with evidence."

"I won't comment on that."

"And I have to find my way through the maze with no help from him, believe it or not."

"I take not."

"I'll see you in court."

"If you insist."

"Not my decision."

"You should have stayed on our side."

"Times I wish I had. This is one of them."

MAX '46 III

THE WEDDING WENT FORWARD ON SATURDAY AFTERNOON AS PLANNED. Barney's secretary and Betsy's called the whole invitation list to make sure everyone knew it was a go. Neither one reported any adverse comments, and the acceptance rate was virtually the same as the original RSVP tally: close to 100 percent. Definitely the party of the season. And it came off impeccably, without a misstep.

Max got someone at the hospital to send a classic, Dallas-scale floral arrangement from him and a congratulatory telegram Barney was asked to read for him. Had Max not made it back against such prohibitive odds, there would have been some mixed emotions, particularly among those who were close to him, but since the word had spread with the help of the *Herald* that he was alive and in Dallas with some prospect of significant recovery, there was no pall over the revels, to which he had reportedly given his blessing.

One disappointed suitor of Betsy's, well in his cups at the party, did make a crack about the Grahams probably having some Jewish blood of their own, given Betsy's strange attraction to it. But a Graham cousin, not quite as far gone, led him onto the lawn behind the main dining room and punched him out, putting an end to that line of banter.

Dorothea had utterly succumbed to Glenn's campaign, as he had to her quiet charm. She and Glenn danced cheek-to-cheek at the reception, the child propped up on his right forearm, her arms tight around his neck, her head cradled between his big shoulder and his cheek, her eyes, when they were open, glistening with joy as he whirled her around the floor. With her approval (and her school's), he

165

and Betsy had decided on a plan to take "their darling girl" on their honeymoon trip to Europe, so that she wouldn't connect Glenn's entry into the family with her first real separation from Betsy.

Betsy, Glenn, and Dorothea were driven home together to the house Max and Betsy had built, and they had a quiet supper in the dining room, before the grown-ups explained that they would delay their honeymoon for a while, at least until Max was clearly on the mend. They spent a little time reviewing the modest changes in routine in the household and assuring the child that her life would only be enhanced by Glenn's presence and the likelihood that he would adopt her formally, with Max's approval. Explaining Max's new role was a bit more challenging, since it hadn't actually been defined. But they assured her she could look at him as a kind of third grandfather, as devoted as the first two.

The child had loved Glenn, almost from the start, and his charming parents had made two trips to Dallas in the previous three months, both with the primary objective of assuring Dorothea that she would become a cherished member of their family, as each of them hoped to become of hers. Whatever concerns, if any, she may have had in the face of these repeated assurances, didn't seem to dim her outlook, and she embraced Betsy and Glenn with what certainly appeared to be love and trust before she went to her own suite to turn in.

DANNY '90 IV

THE INDICTMENT WAS DELIVERED, WITH A COPY TO US, THE FOLLOWING morning. Neither the judge nor I was surprised that it was general to the point of being almost impenetrable. But a few points were clear despite all the absence of specificity. The major charges were insider trading and conspiracy to commit securities fraud, bribery, and money laundering. The legal underpinning was RICO. And the documents seemed to give off a palpable scent of prosecutorial confidence.

The judge had walked around to my office with it as soon as he got the copy I had made for him.

"So, Peter," he said, "now we know they know what we don't and why he's reluctant to acknowledge any of it, even to us. Your buddies over there must be licking their chops."

"On what I knew from other sources, this wasn't remotely where I thought they were going."

"They have to have substance to try this."

"So why work so hard to bring me over? If they've got enough to bring these charges, they shouldn't be worried."

"They're probably not as confident as these papers make them sound."

"I was thinking as I read it, they must be relying heavily on testimony of co-conspirators. Miller is too smart to have left much physical evidence lying around. They may figure between us we can take the witnesses apart."

"I think so, too. But we have to make a decision before our partners' meeting in twenty minutes. What do you want to do? So

167

far as I'm concerned, Peter, it's your call. I won't throw the fight, of course, but I'd love to see the good guys win and Miller take the fall. What do you say?"

"I'm just too biased, Judge. You have to call it."

"As I told you from day one, Peter, the book says take the case and the money. Give him the best defense we can. If their evidence holds up, maybe we lose. That would not be a crying shame."

"You saw what he is."

"Just a smart, rich punk. Not Mengele."

"So what do we have to ask the partners?"

"Nothing," Farkas shrugged. "At least we'll get to hear the stories."

"And if they're not credible or just don't hold up . . . ?"

"Then he walks. Another malefactor beats the system. But worse things have happened. Do you want me to call him?"

"Unless you particularly want to, I'll do it. They'll both like that."

*   *   *

The prosecutor must have released it for the early editions, and the press ate it up. Miller and his lawyer were cool in the face of the first blasts. Danny seemed to be more satisfied that he had succeeded in getting us to represent him than worried about the charges. I asked him, once we were seated again around the same conference table, if he believed they had any hard evidence.

"How do you characterize false witnesses?" he asked.

"If they corroborate each other credibly, it's not bad evidence. Hard to make it a 'smoking gun' in the classic sense, but if it's played right for cumulative effect, it can go a long way."

"But it certainly isn't 'hard evidence,' is it?"

"You can't say that categorically," I answered. And the judge nodded agreement.

Yesterday's big question was no longer the elephant in the room, but it was still relevant. I didn't feel we had much to lose if I asked Miller again, in light of the morning's news, "Do you think it may now be in your interests to tell us any of those stories before we hear them in court?"

"No," he said, "for the same reasons I stated yesterday."

"You don't consider the indictment itself a meaningful change in circumstances, Mr. Miller?" the judge asked.

"No. A model of arrogant consistency. We'll hear what they've cooked up soon enough. Then we'll dissect it, discuss it, and discredit it. Unless you have some other plan," he said.

"Of course," I said, "if we knew what we are likely to hear, we might have some other strategy to recommend. But you're putting us in a position in which we can only counterpunch after they've laid out their evidence. You've effectively closed out anything we might do preemptively."

"I certainly have not!" Miller shot back.

"If you think you haven't, Danny, you may not understand the consequences of your refusal to level with us. We'll presumably begin getting up to speed when they put their first witness on the stand. But we will be playing from behind, and we may never catch up."

McGuiness roused himself and actually addressed me. "I would not have been surprised if the U.S. Attorney had sent in his shock troops to seize Mr. Miller and haul him downtown in handcuffs. And I'm frankly wondering why he passed up that photo op when he could have 'justified' the move by describing our client as a flight risk. Do you have any opinion?"

"That would have given us an argument that he was trying to discredit the defendant in public before he'd presented any evidence of wrongdoing. It's blatant enough that he released the indictment to the press and let them give Miller the black eye themselves," I said. "I'll claim it's a lynching anyway, on those grounds, but it would have made my day if they'd yanked him out in chains."

"How about the RICO maneuver?" Danny himself asked.

"I thought it was seriously overstepping and argued against it when we were starting to develop the Milkin case, and I consider it at least equally inappropriate here. I fought it from inside then, and I'll certainly call them on it, loud and clear here. But they got away with it once, and I guess they figure it's worth a shot here, too. Nevertheless, I think it may work for us."

"Why? Doesn't it help them compel damaging testimony?"

"Yes, but the implicit coercion degrades its value."

"So you'd call it a wash, Peter?"

"Maybe a little better than that, for us. Marginally, perhaps, but I'd say it's in your favor."

"Our favor?"

"Right. Whatever they have, we're probably going to have to attack as contrived, witch-hunting, more coincidence than conspiracy. And the more they play to the crowd, the more we have to work with."

"Now you're talking," Miller said.

"Just remember," I said, "until we know what they have, that's what it is, just talk."

"I'm not asking for guarantees. What I want to hear is an aggressive battle plan, and what you're saying begins to sound like one."

"Danny, you're only hearing what you want to hear. Over the last twenty-four hours, I've also told you some things you didn't want to hear and therefore dismissed, although they were, and are, quite true and certainly relevant."

"Isn't that within my rights?"

"If you think so. But the problem is that your refusal to give us potentially valuable information you have makes it much more difficult to defend you effectively. If we are forced to hear everything they might have for the first time when it's presented in court, we can't attack. All we can do is counterpunch. And that means, even if they miss with some shots, they will land some, and every blow they land builds their case with the jury. If we know what's likely to be thrown at us, we can block some, slip some, get them out of their rhythm. So you're simply undermining your own defense. Don't you see it?"

Miller sat back in his chair, tented his fingertips, and pursed his lips. He waited perhaps a minute before speaking. Then he finally said, "I think you can do it my way. Just focus all of your critical faculties on trying to evaluate the likelihood that what they are claiming is true. You're going to know if it is or it isn't in most instances. If it's bullshit, knock it down. You've heard enough coerced testimony to recognize it when you hear it. Just trust your judgment and challenge what you doubt on cross. You'll know bullshit when you hear it. Trust your own judgment."

I looked over to the judge and shook my head. Farkas gave a little shrug with his shoulders and fingers.

"Danny," I said, "you're smarter than this. We'll study the presentment some more and come back with further questions this afternoon. Then you can give us another pep talk or some answers. It's your game to call. But I have to tell you, some information from you will do a lot more for our fighting spirit than your Knute Rockne act. Let's resume at 1:00 p.m. here."

I excused myself and walked out, just barely checking my temper.

MAX '46 IV

Max's recovery astonished the medical staff at Dallas Methodist. The friends who began to visit him in the hospital suite, with the exception of Barney and Marty, had no real reference points to measure it from, and they saw an aged shadow of the dynamic young man they had known, apparently struggling to regain even a viable portion of his strength and vitality. But the staff and the two insiders would be startled from day to day at the comeback. Within six weeks, Max had been able to dismiss any consideration of his moving on to some rehabilitation facility and was demanding and getting medical permission to visit the houses and apartments the two old friends lined up for him to see.

He was reluctant to accept Betsy and Glenn's invitations to visit them and Dorothea at what had been his home. And he didn't relish the idea of the child coming to see him at the hospital. They met at Barney's home, or the golf club, or Devlin's estate, until Max, after a week of house hunting, bought, handsomely furnished, a sprawling Georgian manor house on the far side of the golf course from his previous home and began ordering in and buying at local shops on his daily rides around town with Devlin, a few of his favorite creature comforts to give it his own stamp.

From then on, the friends and family met at Max's for a while, until the frequency and numbers of the drop-ins and their servicing requirements began to wear down the household staff, and Max put out some feelers about buying a restaurant. In an economy making a limping transition from wartime boom to "normalcy," there were some high-grade prospects on the market at attractive prices. Barney picked a well-known steak house with an even better known bar and bought it on a handshake over lunch with the second-generation owners. The name of the place, by coincidence, was Barney's, and Max decided to keep it that way.

Then his routine began to take shape around tea, fruit, and toast at 6:30 a.m., supervised rehab in his own gym and glass-enclosed swimming pool from 7:00 a.m. to noon, lunch at a big table in the steak house, usually with four or five drop-ins, until midafternoon, then a massage with Barney or Marty, followed by drinks and a light dinner with one of them at the club or his home, and early to bed. In three months, Max looked like a vigorous fifty-five year old, not getting any older in a hurry. It was hard to tell he'd ever been sick, let alone at death's door.

And business opportunities, even in an economy barely staving off recession, just came rolling at him. He reviewed them himself and reached out for special industry expertise when he needed it, as he did in most manufacturing areas where the prospects for future profitability were always presented as grand scale, but as Max saw it, the requirements for specialized, experienced management talent struck him as highly problematic.

After a few weeks of daily presentations, generally over his round table, Max listened to a respectful pitch from two brothers, big, strapping, just mustered out, multiply decorated Seabees who had been small-scale local construction contractors for several years before enlisting the day after Pearl Harbor. They had served together and begun talking two years before about starting a residential development operation if they could line up the right backing.

As soon as they were mustered out, they scouted the area and identified an attractive thousand-acre fruit orchard site, bisected by a stream, a few miles west of the little airport between Dallas and Ft. Worth. They could buy it for $300 an acre (without the mineral rights), on terms, and they had just under $40,000 in savings of their own.

Max liked their intelligence and directness, and their ambition was palpable. He also felt that backing them was the right way to express his gratitude for what they'd done for his adopted country. He asked them if they could handle the entire construction management, including the roads and utilities, and they said they were sure they could, teamed with a successful businessman with capital, banking connections, and some political clout to supplement the modest access they brought to the table as local boys with good war records.

Max told them they had the partner they needed, and that he would bring in, to his share, friends who had any necessary connections he didn't. The brothers asked if he could fund a $20 million program with a maximum peak requirement of $10 million out-of-pocket. And when he said he could, they then asked him about ownership. He proposed investing $5 million as equity, and another $10 million as a line of credit, for 60 percent of "this first project" and an option to finance the equity required for everything they wanted to do thereafter, until he passed on two offers.

The brothers said Max had a deal, if he liked the property. Max stood up, as they did, and the three partners shook hands, saying they'd get it papered up as soon as possible, mutually promising to keep it simple. Then they asked him if he'd like to see the orchard site, and when Max said yes, they all drove out in his car that afternoon. He liked what he saw and heard and liked the McCarthy boys even more. They signed the contract three days later.

Max called Barney and Marty Devlin late the following morning, as soon as he finished his rehab routine, and asked them to stop by the restaurant for a private lunch meeting if they could arrange their schedules on that short notice. They were both at his place at 12:30 and Max had the three of them seated in a quiet corner, giving the big table a pass for the day.

He described the brothers and the property, briefly and accurately. Barney said he knew the McCarthy family from way back and that they were solid citizens. He also said he knew the boys were considered legitimate war heroes. Max told his friends they could join him in the deal on any scale they wanted up to half his share between them, and asked if they'd like to visit the property that afternoon. Devlin said he was in for whatever share Max thought was right, site unseen, and Barney said he'd take whatever Devlin didn't, provided he liked the property, and he was ready to go look at it that day.

Max said he had a hunch the brothers might be out at the orchard and he'd leave a message at their little office in Dallas in any event. The three of them were on the road, in Barney's car, before the table was cleared. They reminisced and kidded each other all the way to the site, each of them saying, in his own way, that this was the best day they'd had since Max left on his mission.

The brothers caught up with them on the site and talked about why they liked its gently rolling hills, the stream, and the greening effects of the orchard, much of which they wanted to preserve, and how they wanted to develop it as a planned community with homes selling in a price range from $50,000 to $100,000, on lot sizes of three-quarters to one-and-a-half acres and common spaces taking 20 percent, roads and streets another 10 percent. They were projecting 600 homes at an average price of $75,000, total revenues of some $45 million from sales, and a gross profit pretax over three years of just over $15 million on the $5 million cash equity investment, plus the bank-funded line of credit of another $10 million.

Bob, the elder brother, said he was sure they could pick up enough frontage on the nearby county road to build a small retail area as the "village" center for convenience shopping (the two terms hadn't yet been regularly conjoined as "shopping center"), but all five of them could see that the development would have to satisfy that requirement. Bob said he and his brother didn't know much about the retail business, but Max and Marty assured them they did.

Barney said he understood that the McCarthy brothers would own 40 percent of the deal and expressed his own preference that they put their own money on the line, too. Bob said they could put up $40,000, but that would mean they had to begin drawing salaries against their potential profit interests from the start to feed the families they would be starting. Barney asked them if a thousand a month apiece in cash compensation would do it for openers until there was some funds flow from home sales and retail rentals. The brothers said that . . . amount would work for them unless prices began to take off without the wartime controls. They all agreed there'd be adjustments in that case.

Marty then pulled Max and Barney off to the side for a minute and proposed that either the three of them take equal shares of the 60 percent allocated to Max, or, if Max preferred, he could retain 30 percent and Barney and Marty would come down to 15 percent apiece. Max immediately said he was "fine" with their splitting the 60 percent, 20-20-20 "straight-up."

The three of them agreed on the equal shares of the majority interest, then walked back over to the brothers with their hands outstretched to shake on a deal they would immediately reduce to contract. For that moment, in the spirit of the agreement, there was no discussion of the terms of the credit line, but it was clear they all knew they'd work it out.

"What do you want to call this deal?" Max asked them all. Then before he had answers from them, he suggested "The Orchards" for the development and "Orchard Development Company" for their operating entity. All hands agreed.

He then told the brothers they should feel free to discuss anything with any of the three "elders," but that when they needed a quick decision, they should go right to Devlin because he, as the busiest of the three of them, would be the one they could count on to pay attention, make quick decisions, and keep his friends in line and on board.

*   *   *

Max had just finished his morning rehab session and come out of the shower when his houseman knocked on the door of his bedroom and asked if he could come in.

Max, still toweling, told the man to enter, and he did, looking a bit less poised than usual. "There's someone downstairs to see you, sir."

"Who is it?"

"He didn't say, sir. Only that he was an old friend."

"Did he look like an old friend?"

"I couldn't say that, sir."

"What are you worried about, Richard? Does he look like he bites?"

"No, sir. But the way he speaks, he sounds like he might."

"I have an idea who that could be," Max said. "Make him comfortable in the library. Offer him anything he wants and tell him I'll be down in a few minutes. Say I'm sorry to keep him waiting."

Richard said, "Yes, sir," just avoided clicking his heels, and went off to settle the visitor.

Max put on a sport shirt, slacks, and a tweed jacket, moccasins, no socks, and was downstairs heading into the library in less than five minutes.

"Is that you, Carlo?" he called out into the library from the bottom of the stairs.

"You bet it is, Duke," the visitor called back in the voice that upset Richard.

Max entered. Carlo Marchetti crossed the room to embrace him, and the two hugged each other like father and son, both of them just holding back tears.

"What's this bullshit about you being so sick?"

"Overplayed," Max said, still hugging the older man. "I was just a little knocked out. But I'm doing fine."

"Good for you, you tough little bastard, but you nearly got me and some of your nearest and dearest killed on account of you disappeared."

Max pushed him back down in lounge chair and held his head between his hands. "Why would anybody want to rough you up because I had to do something I had to do that was none of their business?"

"Get me a drink and a cigar, and I'll tell you all about it."

"Richard didn't offer you anything?"

"He did," Carlo said, "but he was so nervous I told him to take a walk."

Max stepped to the drinks tray, poured Carlo a Napoleon brandy, and brought it to him, along with a small humidor he flipped open, a silver cup full of wooden matches and a cigar clipper. Then he sat down himself and said, "OK, Mr. Real Tough Guy, make me laugh."

Marchetti made a fuss over clipping and lighting the cigar, smiled at the fragrance, and took a sip of the brandy before releasing the smoke. "Not bad, kid," he said, winking at his protégé.

"*Manongia mia,* it's good to see you, the Duke of Max. I can't believe it, I tell you."

"Are you going to keep playing foxy Grandpa, or tell me the story?"

"First, you tell me why you didn't even let me know what you were doing."

"I left a message with your office."

"That you had to take a trip?"

"I did."

"That really helped, then you're gone seven years, and I don't hear word one. Thanks."

"It was a little tough getting postcards out from where I was."

"How about before you went? You leave a fucking message? You can't tell me the story, where you're going, what you're trying to do. Like who the hell am I? How could I possibly be any help? What do I need to know, just another old Guido?"

"I knew what you'd say. The same thing everybody else said. 'Don't do it.' I didn't want to hear it, Carlo. I had to go."

"Did you do any good?"

"Probably ten million got slaughtered, mostly Jews. I slipped maybe sixty out that probably would have been killed. Compared to what I did to people here who loved me, also my people, my flesh and blood, I'm not so sure it adds up to anything special, bottom line, except for those few dozen. I'm just lucky the ones I left here are all right."

"You're not lucky you're all right?"

"Compared to what could have been, I certainly was. Very lucky. But come on, tell me the story."

"You could figure it out if you thought about it. But I'll tell you some, just to give you a better idea."

"Good. Shoot."

"Oh yeah, that's what it almost came to."

"You're kidding."

"I don't kid about this kind of shit. By the time you left, eight of the most ungrateful bastards in the USA had been making and cleaning big money through you and making legitimate fortunes on top of that for five years."

"They weren't laundering money through me. That never was my business."

"Max, I know what your first business was. Banging around deadbeats for us. Laundering money would have been a big step up. But anyway, what's the difference? You were making clean, rich, fucking taxpaying Boy Scouts out of the worst criminals in the country for years with your oil shit, and like they always do, they were entitled to have it go on forever, the way they saw it. So when you left, you took away something they figured was theirs. Forget how much money you'd made them. In their book, what you hadn't made them yet was also theirs.

"Like Giancana said to me when I tried to explain, 'Bullshit, it's over. When we're selling protection to some manufacturer, and he dies of natural causes, we give his wife and kids a home-free pass? The fuck we do. The family keeps paying or we put 'em in the hospital for a few months, and when they get out we're the senior partners in the firm. They don't understand that, we put 'em in the cemetery. You know the rules.'"

"Not Max's family," I say. "He paid his dues. He wants to do something else now," I tell him. "He does it. He earned it. He's out."

"Nobody walks on us," Giancana says. "Nobody's ever out."

"You telling me that, Sam?" I say.

"I'm fucking telling you, Carlo. Nobody ever walks away from us. You're in with us, we own you and yours. Period. Nobody walks. Anybody tries, we break his legs so he can forget about walking. Then if he's still too dumb to understand, we cut his balls off and stuff 'em down his throat. Whether he's Max Landsberg or Carlo Marchetti or any other fuck.

"So you go take care of it, Carlo, and fast. Or you get the same treatment. Nobody walks."

"I make a snap decision. I know the old rules. I don't try to change 'em. I try another tack. I got to find a way to sell him you're dead as Kelsey's and your family's out of reach.

"So I tell Sammy, I'm gonna do what I can. Sammy tells me I'm gonna do what he tells me. He don't wanna know what I can do, unless it's what he says.

"Then I hear you got a bunch of Jews together in Marseille. Trying to get 'em on a boat to Cuba. And the next thing I hear you're trying to get them over the Spanish border. Then the Spaniards pick you up and turn you over to the Germans. And the Germans are suddenly big buddies with the Russkies, so they turn you over to them. And that's all she wrote. Nobody knows nothing. You just disappear, maybe become a commissar. Who knows? Nobody knows. You're just gone.

"So it dawns on me. Get the word back to Sammy you're dead. Executed by the Russians as a Jewish spy, after they got all your money pretending to help you get your lantsmen out. So what's the point of trying to squeeze you? You're finished. And your family don't have any money because you threw it all away trying to save your Jews.

"And Giancana's got other things on his plate. What did Buggsy do with the Las Vegas money? Is this prick Batista gonna play ball in Havana? Is that crazy Trafficante gonna make a play for the whole thing, our thing? He ain't even Italian, that spic. And Sammy's using dope big time to take his mind off his troubles. He can't fucking think straight. He's probably forgot about you. Which it turns out he has. You're yesterday's agita, and so am I. Fogeddabout it. He don't even know Betsy's alive, God knows not Dorothea. The heat's off unless Giancana wakes up, which ain't likely enough to worry about, fucked up like he is.

"And that's how it played. But believe me, I was scared shitless, crazy as that bastard is. Worried he's gonna take the cure and wake up, come looking for me and your family just to prove nobody walks.

"As luck has it, he don't. If he does wake up straight any day, all he can think of is broads. McGuire broads. Exner. Whatever.

"You're last week, last month. He can't even remember yesterday. A fag named Rosselli is running the show from Key Biscayne. The word is Sammy has a crush on him. Case closed. My bullshit story about you being dead is OK. You just don't matter. The whole bunch is making so much money from dope and gambling, they can't even remember the oil business.

"Big fucking joke. Very funny. But I know how close it was. Believe me, you don't wanna know, *that's* how close it was. You're better off dead, just in case. Your family's OK.

"Fogeddabout it. Everything is under control. Then you fucking turn up alive. I gotta consider getting you knocked off in the hospital, which ain't so tough 'cause that's where most people go to die anyway. I sit tight for a while; maybe it'll blow over. Then I fly down to get the lay of the land here, and you're fucking Charles Atlas again. I don't need this, Duke, my boy. If I had any brains, I'd put out a contract on you before the news gets around and we're both on the hit list.

"What have you got to say for yourself, my fancy friend?"

"I love you, you old bastard. Let those hopheads come for us. If they get us, they get us. I'm happy to go out with you. You're the best. But they'd better be very good. Or they'll be the ones sleeping with the fishes. We don't die easily, Carlo and his boy, Max." He stood up and walked over to Carlo, put his hands on the sides of the older man's face again. "Forget about it."

"You don't even remember how to say it," Carlo said.

"I never was a real wop, remember?"

"No, just a Jew imitation."

"Yes. Meyer and I. Fake wops."

"You should live so. You and Meyer? You got some nerve, Duke."

DANNY '90 V

THE JUDGE AND I HAD TO CONCLUDE THAT, AT LEAST UNTIL WE GOT into the courtroom, Miller was going to stick to his guns and let us be surprised by what we heard there. His stance put us at a major, immediate disadvantage in the *voir dire*. We could make some reasonable assumptions about attitudes from color and ethnicity, occupation, education, attire, appearance, visible response to authority, apparent level of interest in the case, and readiness to serve on the panel. But trying to guess about potentially crucial experiences and prejudices without knowing what they might hear seemed a pointless exercise and not worth the inevitable risk of antagonizing someone who would end up being impaneled.

We took a few shots on classic grounds and used up our challenges, as the prosecution did with their massive advantage of knowing just what the jurors would hear, and we assumed they ended up with a "better jury" than we did. Given that presumption, we really couldn't understand why the prosecution delayed until the last possible minute before providing the list of its witnesses. They had to assume Miller was giving us the information we needed, and their tactical game didn't seem to be worth the candle.

But when we did get the list, we made sure Miller reviewed it thoroughly and went through the drill of asking him what he imagined those witnesses would testify to under oath.

"None of these people can truthfully say anything that would be damaging to me," he insisted.

"Do you know these people, Danny?"

"A few, I do."

"There are twenty-one people on this list, Danny. How many do you know?"

He picked up his copy of the witness list, traced his right index finger down the page, and finally said, "Six."

"The other fifteen you know nothing about?"

"I recognize a few of the names."

"But you haven't had anything to do with them?"

"Some of them may be in the investment business, one way or another, and I could have run across them or met them at some time or other."

"Do you recognize any of those names as being the names of persons or being associated with persons who might have some reason to give false testimony against you?"

"No, but who knows what people can be pressured to do. All I can tell you is that none of them can give truthful testimony that would be damaging to me."

Judge Farkas broke in. "Mr. Miller, is it possible that you believe the appearance of your defense counsel being genuinely surprised by some testimony provided by a prosecution witness or witnesses could work in your favor?"

"I hadn't considered that possibility," Danny said.

"Please answer my question, Mr. Miller," the judge said.

"I just did, Mr. Farkas."

The judge turned to me, palms open. "No further questions, Counselor," he said. "I'm sure the court would give us some time to investigate this list, if we asked for it, given the extraordinarily late service." Then he looked at his watch and said, again to me, "We'd better be going downtown. We'll get there faster by subway."

And we took the six downtown, all four of us, presumably leaving Danny's driver to find his way to Foley Square on his own. Danny offered the only open seat in the subway car to Farkas, who declined it. I walked a few steps away to take a strap of my own, which is really how I thought about it, in Virginia Woolf terms. I had no interest in whatever any of the three of them might say over the next few minutes. I wanted to chew on the irony, all alone, for a few minutes.

No reputable law firm should be prepared to represent Danny Miller in a trial of this nature. Even without my special knowledge, any good securities lawyer could figure out Danny the Green Dragon. He represents everything loathsome about Wall Street. Smart, gutsy little miscreants using their unwholesome gifts to take money from the accounts of less clever, but probably much more decent people, and get it transferred to their own.

For our firm to represent him places us on the same rung of the ethical ladder he occupies. Are we in any way ethically, morally superior to him? Can we make any credible claim to higher standards than his? Not on what I've seen over the past few months. We are the zero-sum paragons of the law.

Our duty is to the customer. He pays the bill; we deliver the merchandise. A little frayed around the edges, but just what the customer ordered. We are professionals. We play hardball, and we give every client, make that any client, the best representation money can buy.

That doesn't make us sluts. God forbid. Prostitutes, maybe, but not sluts. At $400 to $1,000 an hour for full partners, we sure as hell don't give any nooky away. The canons say that's our duty, best representation, and God knows, we do it. Officers of the court, obligations to uphold. Come on, look around the room when court is in session. Does the army of the law look outgunned to you? They really don't need our help, not with all their resources.

But how does the formidable Alvin Emil Zola Farkas feel about the spot he's in, knowing what he now knows, let alone what he suspects, about Danny Miller? I look over to him, half a subway car away. He certainly is standing straight. I wouldn't put too much stock in the slight crinkling of his nostrils as if he'd just smelled something dead or dying. The MTA cleaning crews are not highly motivated. Maybe they've missed something. Or maybe it's the smell of the position he's walked us into that's getting to him. It sure is getting to me.

If we do manage to beat the rap for Danny Miller, we'll have won one for the gypper, not the Gipper. If we don't get him off, we look like incompetents, losing a major white-collar crime case before a packed house.

We emerged at Chambers and walked over to the federal courthouse as if we'd taken a vow of silence. There were several reporters and cameramen waiting at the foot of that grand flight of steps, but they accepted being brushed off without the comments they sought. If there were any hecklers, I didn't hear them. And we made it through security reasonably quickly.

I could feel that the judge, as much as I, would have loved to have an alternative to walking into Room 200. Miller wasn't exactly chipper, but he had his head up, shoulders back, ready for battle, and McGuiness was taking his cue from the client.

Federal District Court Judge Anthony DiPalma had been a U.S. Attorney himself, and after twelve distinguished years on the federal bench, he had the quiet command jurists with his background project. No show. No nonsense. "This is my Court. I do know the law, and I apply it as I see fit. Test me at your peril." Ergo, we had a competent judge.

Farkas stared straight-ahead, looking much older than his sixty-eight years. Was he feeling the weight of having taken the bait?

And there was Danny Boy, surrounded by his lawyers, at the defense table. Poised, alert, ready to go, wearing a slight, wry smile. Bring it on. Clearly, we had a defendant looking ready to go. And we had defense counsel, buffed but not really briefed, a good deal less ready to go. And after just one day of not very hotly contested *voir dire*, we had a jury of Miller's purported peers, plus two alternates.

The prosecution, of course, we had in spades. The deputy U.S. Attorney himself, looking insufferably pleased. Two experienced senior assistants, clearly not unhappy to be on the case. And, in and out, always moving at high speed, with impressive senses of urgency, three lesser assistants I had identified so far. The bell was about to sound. Not for the first time that morning, I felt a sharp twist of anguish about being on the wrong side and not having the nerve to pay the career costs of switching back.

What we didn't have, and could definitely have used, as events would prove, was an experienced referee licensed by the New York State Boxing Commission, duly empowered to declare a fight no contest.

MAX '47-'67

MAX WAS WELL AWARE OF THE MOB MAXIM THAT NO ONE WALKS away without Carlo's warning "reminder." And he thought through the undoubtedly well-meant advice. But his own well-meaning miscalculations, which he had to acknowledge had led him to a disastrous, nearly fatal, misadventure in 1939, had made him more respectful of the role of chance in human affairs. Odds were just probability computations, and while they would be very likely to govern outcomes if players could stay at the table indefinitely, they were far from accurately predictive of outcomes in single instances. And the downside of some risks made even highly favorable odds unacceptable.

His risk/reward analysis of the possibility that the mob would discover on its own that he was alive and back in the U.S. made it one of those risks that were unacceptable, by his reckoning, because he knew that the supposed rule against pursuing vendetta against family was frequently suspended when a capo chose to ignore it. His answer to the dilemma was to go beard the lion.

He arrived in Chicago a week later, having called to apologize to Carlo, override his resistance, and ask him to tell Sam Giancana he was coming specifically to see him, at the capo's convenience. Giancana sent back word that he would see Max at his office, and set a time. Max arrived half an hour early, *di rispetto,* and waited in a rococo reception area until he was called into the sanctum twenty minutes late.

The boss came around from behind his desk to throw his arms around Max and tell him he looked like a million dollars, "especially

186

after what I heard you went through." He did not offer his ring to kiss.

Max knew Giancana was the incarnation of mercurial, but he played along with the warm reception and respectfully returned the compliment, staying acutely alert to any hint of resentment or anger, as "Sam" (the boss insisted) led him to a seat opposite his desk and walked back to his chair behind it.

"I know Halladay kept working with my friends while I was away," Max said, "and I was happy to learn you and your friends did well with those ventures in my absence, as I knew you would. Now that I'm back alive and reasonably well, I wanted to see you both to apologize for not speaking to you myself before I had to leave and to assure you that I will keep a close eye on your oil and gas interests again. As I did before."

"You set it up great, Maxey. You're a smart cookie, even though you maybe went off your rocker a little just before the war. No hard feelings. No losses, continuing good profits. Nothing to make up. I appreciate the apology, and I accept it. I understand loyalty to your people, even when others might say it goes too far. *La famiglia e la famiglia, siempre,* eh?"

Max nodded sagely. "No one knows better than you, Sam."

"You're a hundred percent right, Max. You still got that good head on your shoulders, kiddo. Now make sure you keep it there. I'm glad to have you back. Anything I can do for you, you let me know. So just keep the ball rolling and stay in touch. Anything comes up, I'll reach out to you through my *paisan,* Carlo." He touched two fingers of his right hand to his forehead and looked down at the papers on his desk.

Max took the signal, rose, said, "*Grazie tanto, Don Samuelo,*" made a half bow, turned, and walked out, opening the door for himself, still wondering if he had really made the peace, knowing he'd find out sooner or later. Back in his hotel suite, he called Marchetti, who picked up the line himself, on the first ring.

"I met with Sam for a few minutes this morning, Carlo."

"Like I don't know that."

"I'm not surprised you do."

"And?"

"Of course, I don't really know the man."

"If you did, you wouldn't. Nobody does."

"But if I can believe what he said, he has no beef with me."

"He said that?"

"Yes. Can I believe him?"

"Let's say it's a start that he wants you to think so. You walked back to your hotel?"

"Yes."

"There was a very good chance you wouldn't have been able to do that, Duke."

"He really does want the oil program to keep going."

"I imagine so. He's still making good money. I know because I have my beak in there for a little bit, too. But since it was just as good while you were away, I knew he might think he could do without you now, too, which would leave him a no-cost whack, just for spite."

"He didn't seem to have that in mind."

"You really think you can read Sammy G? Forget it. But we might as well hope you're right. If you're not on the hit list, I'm probably not either, and your family is probably OK. You'll only know that for sure the day you die in your bed of natural causes.

"But take my advice now, for Christ's sake, and get out of town today. Today, you hear me? He drinks in the afternoon, sometimes more than he can handle, and he can be one mean drunk, let me tell you. Out of sight is out of mind, which is exactly where you should be.

"And I'm gonna take a little trip to the old country, too, as of right now. I don't want to be within easy reach if his mood changes, which it has a way of doing anytime, anywhere. Get going. Have a good trip home, and count your blessings. *Ciaou, ragazzo mio,*" Carlo rang off before Max could answer.

But Max took his advice this time, was home in Dallas that night, and didn't return to Illinois for nearly five years. When he did, it was by invitation from Betsy and Glenn to attend the party celebrating the engagement of Dorothea to another scion of a wealthy Chicago family that had founded and still controlled a major securities firm, strong enough to survive the Depression and flourish during and after WWII. The wedding would take place in Dallas, where Betsy and Glenn lived part of the year, and the engagement party siting in Chicago was a nod to the lakeshore connections on both sides.

Max was delighted with the way his daughter had developed into a lovely, graceful young woman, and a budding beauty, but he had reservations about the groom, whose striking good looks and extraordinary confidence in his own charm left the extra "grandfather" with some uneasiness about the youngster's staying power as a man and a husband.

Max had been unfailingly loving, generous, and supportive with Dorothea (now Dorothy, at her own insistence), but in his bow to the unusual nature of the relationship, never forceful in expressing his opinions unless specifically, and unmistakably, solicited. He hoped she knew she could count on him, in any circumstance, yet he was acutely aware that he'd never been put to the test on a matter of any consequence, as Barney, too discreet to tell him, undoubtedly had.

The prospective groom was "correct" with Max, adequately respectful, as well, but Max, always alert to subtleties, sensed that the young man felt he had some "inside" knowledge about him that gave him an implicit superiority. He also knew that there were still enough survivors around from the old days to make it likely that a rigorous background check by a well connected lawyer for a prominent Cook County family could find some sources who would tie the smart, gutsy young Max Landsberg to the smooth, elegant, and obviously wealthy "Duke" Landers, despite all appearances to the contrary. Thus, the young man's veiled but detectable superciliousness didn't really surprise Max, and he took it without displaying any hint of irritation.

The party was a widely reported social event and apparently a success. The press did not mention Max among the bride-to-be's family members, and he returned to Dallas the next day by scheduled airliner, fully focused on his thriving business interests and investments.

He did have one brief discussion with Barney about the couple over lunch at the golf club that summer and was interested to note that Barney had his own reservations about the boy, which he attributed to his youth, looks, and social position, but felt that Dorothy could probably handle him and knows enough to call for help if she found she couldn't.

Max stayed in touch with Dorothy by telephone, attended the grand-scale Dallas wedding, and made the couple a handsome, six-figure gift. His contact with them became more and more occasional, because the couple was living in Chicago, where Dorothy got a bachelor's degree and an MFA at Hutchins very prestigious university (then riding high) while her husband earned an MBA at Kellogg and a law degree at Northwestern before settling full-time into the family brokerage and investment business, Miller Securities.

When the young couple's first child, a healthy boy, was born shortly after Dorothy received her MFA, Max and Barney each set up well funded new trusts for her and her children and were very pleased to learn that all of the grandparents had made similar moves. They all had heard that Gary was "doing exceptionally well" in the securities business, and Dorothy was following her mother's path in the interior design field with a leading Chicago firm to which she returned after a year's maternity leave.

By all reports, the young socialites were thriving happily and certainly suffering no financial strains. As the years passed, Max began to question his initial mistrust of the young man, and Barney had even earlier revised his assessment of the fellow and began to see him as "all right."

By the late-fifties, the American economy was booming as never before, and Max's various businesses, particularly his oil and real estate interests, were pushing him onto lists where he had no desire to appear, as the builder and possessor of one of the country's notable new fortunes. To his increasing concern, no one, certainly not Giancana or Gary's family, had to make any strenuous efforts to get a sense of The Duke's wealth. And Barney, though much less diversified, wasn't very far behind him.

Then suddenly the idyll ended. With no warning that reached Max or Barney in advance, they learned from Betsy and Glenn that Gary had been discreetly supporting a succession of mistresses for years until one of them upped the ante to full recognition, or a substantial seven-figure buy off, and when he did not comply, acted on her threat to tell her stories about herself and her cohorts to Dorothy.

Dorothy, reportedly learning about her husband's double life for the first time, was initially stunned and embarrassed, then, very shortly, furious and bitterly demanding a divorce. They had moved from downtown to lakeshore estate country several years before, Gary commuting to his downtown office and Dorothy running her practice from her home. With the distance providing cover, Gary had begun to relax his guard and be seen around the city with his doxies.

As usual, Dorothy was the last to know, not a single one of her friends having chosen to give her the reports or tell her the gossip. She was implacable. Lawyers, detectives, changed locks, no negotiations, petitions, visitation denial, reparations demands even the successful playboy broker could only meet with his parents' substantial financial help, first refused with indignation, then quickly committed to keep the reputational damage within recoupable proportions.

Their son was twelve and much more coldly, quietly, just as furious as his mother, with no effective outlet, no means of retaliation, except to renounce his father totally and urge his mother to destroy him if she could. while Gary himself didn't even try to justify his behavior to his son any more than he had to his wife. He took the Henry Ford II stance, "never explain, never complain." In his own mind, it seemed, he had just done what men do, when they can.

Dorothy could not in fact, "destroy" her philandering betrayer. And, other than financially, where she did ultimately win a major settlement, for the era, reportedly among the biggest then known in Illinois, she couldn't really hurt him. Gary didn't care enough to be emotionally vulnerable, and he was heard to say later, more than once, and to many, that he never lost a client over the scandal and never would as long as he made money for them.

When he agreed to the settlement, he also agreed not to contest the divorce, deny, or attempt to mitigate his serial adultery, in any manner. But Dorothy wouldn't leave the state, wouldn't leave Lake

Forest until the last document was signed and the money and all common property had changed hands. The boy went to school every day, throughout the process. He did everything he was supposed to do, except appear in court, although the judge ordered him there twice, the second time on pain of a contempt citation. Holding a twelve-year-old charged with no crime in contempt after what he had experienced in his home? Judge Hoffman, arrogant and headstrong, but no fool, relented, before the afternoon editions went to press.

Max and Barney were on the early-morning American flight from Dallas to Chicago the day after Betsy told them the news. They had arranged for a car and driver to take them to Lake Forest and were sitting over tea with Dorothy in the library overlooking her English garden by midafternoon. Dorothy was making a substantial and largely successful effort to appear composed, but she looked to both of them a decade older than her actual early thirties. Still lovely and even able to summon up a bit of self-deprecating humor. No longer the dewy beauty she had been a week before, yet arguably, to the mature observer, even more compelling.

She asked if they could dispense with a detailed review of the still limited information she had and offered to provide them with a summary when the results of the full investigation were available. But she did tell them she appreciated their support and wanted their advice on four subjects: how hard to press her extreme financial demands, how to deal with her son's bitterness, whether to continue to live in Lake Forest or the Chicago vicinity, and whether to persevere in her determination to continue using the locally revered Miller surname for herself and her son. On the latter three points, she reminded them that the boy was just a few months into the current school year and, despite his fury, reportedly continuing to do well academically and athletically.

"For myself, if I were alone, I'd leave this area tomorrow and never look back," she said. "Everything I might have considered worth remembering has been corrupted by the knowledge that I was being played for a fool all along. But I think Daniel's condition is probably more fragile than he'll admit, or perhaps even knows, and the psychiatrist I'm consulting agrees that's likely—although he's only known us for a few days, and Danny, so far, won't agree to see his father or discuss him. So it's essentially my assessment, but I'd like to shield him from any further abrupt changes for a while, if I can. And if he ever decides he wants to change his name, he can always do that himself when he's old enough."

Barney answered after a pause, "I think that's using good judgment, sweetheart, although I'd like to spend some time with Danny, and also your lawyer, before you take that as firm advice."

Max nodded his agreement. "I'd say go with your feel for the situation. You're very close, and you certainly know him better than anyone else."

"I'm not so sure if anyone knows what Daniel is thinking most of the time. He really keeps his own counsel and has since he was a small boy. It's a bit uncanny, but that's the fact," she responded.

"When do you expect him home?" Max asked.

"After soccer practice, probably about 6:30 when he's dropped off here."

"Shall we stay for dinner?" Barney asked.

"Please," she said, "That's what I've planned. And I hope you haven't checked into a hotel. I'd love to have you stay here, but I can't remember if I said that to you, my dears. You brought your bags with you, I know, so perhaps we did agree on that yesterday. I'm a little vague, still. Aftershock, my doctor says."

"Of course," Barney answered. "And we did discuss it yesterday."

"As long as we can be useful, darling," Max added.

At Dorothy's suggestion, the three of them had taken a break for naps in their respective rooms from five to six, and then assembled back in the library for drinks and to await Danny. Dorothy sent the houseman back to other chores and let Barney make the drinks, scotches-on-the rocks for the grandfathers, an extra dry vodka Gibson for her. And when they'd settled, Max asked if Dorothy had any further thoughts she might want to share with them about Danny.

She said there were a few and began with her prioritized concerns. "I believe he is so angry with his father that he's afraid to talk about it because he'd lose control of himself if he did. And Danny is almost obsessed with control, with getting it and keeping it. So it's very difficult to talk him into therapy, even with a psychiatrist renowned for getting smart kids to spill their guts."

Max answered, "Maybe it's something that will just pass with time. The whole problem is, after all, brand-new to him, I assume."

"I'm not sure of that. I think he did have some inkling, or believes he did."

"But aside from his beating himself up, what's so worrisome about his being furious over something that should make him angry?" Barney asked.

"He is acting out his anger. His coach and the assistant principal have both reported complaints from parents that he's taking it out on the other wrestlers. The kids, the coach, the parents, and the administration are all worried that he will hurt one of the boys severely. You know he's much better than anybody else in his weight class."

"In his grade."

"Probably in the state, in the boys fourteen and under class, maybe the sixteen and under juniors, although he hasn't officially wrestled in that class."

"And?" Max asked.

"He's just beating the hell out of everybody he goes in with and really did hurt one of them before the coach could stop the match. Now the parents as well as the kids are complaining to anyone they can get to listen. The coaches won't let him wrestle other boys in the school because he seems so rough, without actually breaking the rules. He's already cracked one boy's forearm by just flipping him so hard. They don't want to let him in with any more kids, so they have him wrestle the assistant coach, and that fellow can barely defend himself against Daniel's aggressiveness. The principal has called him in twice and warned him, and me, directly, about a suspension or expulsion if he injures anyone else."

"Is he starting fights?"

"No, but some of the kids are definitely afraid of him."

"Any trouble with his schoolwork?"

"No. He's a top student in all his courses."

"Still, now?"

"I haven't heard anything to the contrary."

"Behavior in class?"

"No mention of trouble. But I know children are often seriously distressed while a divorce is going on. And I can see how tight he is."

Barney joined, "How hard do you think we should push to take the measure of him?"

"Not hard, please. I think you can ask questions but not push them. If he wants to talk, encourage him, but don't try to force it."

"We'll go easy," Barney reassured her.

Max said, "Don't worry, darling."

The two men took a walk through the garden while Dorothy made some calls. Danny came home earlier than expected, and when he learned from his mother that his Dallas grandfathers were there, he went straight out to find and hug both of them. Max, automatically assessing physical strength as he always did, was impressed by the power of the boy's hug and delighted to see him grinning his welcome.

"In or out, big fella?" Barney asked.

"I'll walk around with you, if you want some more air, Gramps," Danny said agreeably.

And they continued to stroll together, with Danny pointing out, proudly, the latest features of his mother's lovely garden, including a new late-blooming rose variety that had taken a prize at the previous summer's town garden show. Max noted that the boy's arms were exceptionally long for his probably less-than-average height and that he moved along the uneven terrain off the walkway with easy athletic grace while leaving the level ground to them.

"I'm happy to see you in such good spirits, considering what's going on around here," Barney said.

"I'm happy to see some real men around here, too, that's why, Grandpas. And let me tell you, so is Mom. It's just great that you came, and I hope you're going to stay a while."

"If you're up to playing a little golf with two old-timers, let's get out there this weekend. What do you say?"

"I haven't played golf since last summer, although I play tennis pretty much year-round. But I'm game if you are, and it doesn't snow. Only let's not look for a fourth unless Mom wants to come. It'd be great to be just us."

"Any way you like it, Danny. And I'll see to it the champ here gives us both the proper number of strokes."

Max, thinking, missed the cue.

"You heard me, you old hustler, didn't you?"

Max, catching up: "As long as we adjust at the turn."

"Deal," said Danny.

"Did I hear an attempt at a retrade from the original Mr. Deal Is a Deal?"

"You did not. That is the deal."

Danny laughed out loud. "This is going to be great," he said, nearly skipping along sideways.

"I just thought you should see how this shark operates, that's all," Barney said, shaking his head in resignation.

"Are you up to talking with us a few minutes on what's been going on here, Danny?" Max asked.

"Sure, if you want," Danny answered, and he followed them back into the library.

When they arrived, Dorothy ceded them the room, told them dinner would be served at 7:30 to give the grown-ups a chance for cocktails first, and then went up to her own quarters.

The two grandfathers and Danny spread themselves around in comfortable chairs near the fireplace. By unspoken agreement, Barney and Max chose not to start drinking while they were talking with Danny, and Barney opened softly:

"As I said, Daniel, you seem to be handling this miserable situation very well, but Max and I felt it might be helpful if you could tell us how you really feel about it. Just among the three of us, strictly confidentially."

"Yes, sir," Danny said, noticeably less relaxed.

"Dan," Max said, leaning in, "no reason to be on guard with us. We're all in this together. You have to know we're absolutely on your side, so just let it flow."

"Well," Danny offered, "I know you know the story by now. So you can imagine, I'm pretty angry about it."

"At whom and why, in particular, son?" Max asked softly.

"My father, that rat. Mom is just a victim. She's a great lady and a great mother. From anything I ever saw or heard, I believe she was a great wife, too. She's the best; he's the worst. After what he's done to her and to me, to all of us, I don't want to have anything to do with him. In fact, I'd like to take him apart."

"Danny," Barney picked up, "if you do see him, and you undoubtedly will, please don't even think of doing that. If you did, and I imagine you probably could, please don't consider harming him physically or even threatening him. That could be very damaging to your mother's case and to her emotionally. She'd feel responsible and might even be legally held responsible if anything like that happened, since you're a minor under her care right now."

Danny sat silently for a minute, and they let him take his time. After a minute, very tensely, he said "OK, but keep him away from me."

"We'll do everything we can, but we can't promise that while the divorce is pending," Max said. "We can make every effort to be on the scene whenever he is, unless the judge orders otherwise. But on the subject of fighting, there is something else we should talk about."

"I can guess, Grandpa."

"Go ahead."

"I can't keep hurting guys on the mat, or really anywhere else. One, it's not their fault, any of it. They don't have anything to do with it, in the first place, and none of them would dare to tease me about it. I can tell they're on my side, just the way they are with any other kids whose parents are getting divorced. So it isn't fair to take it out on them. Besides that, I'll get expelled if anybody else gets hurt and it even looks a little bit like I did it to them."

"Good. You've got the picture. But would you also like to talk to somebody properly trained to help people through spots like this? It's not an uncommon phenomenon, and there are very good people who can help talk things out and put them in perspective."

"Mom's been suggesting it, therapy, that is. And if I think it could help, I'll let her know, OK?"

"It can. Believe me, and just say the word. If you want to discuss it with us, either of us or both of us, alone, just pass the word."

"You believe in that stuff, I guess?"

Max said yes, and Barney waved his right hand, palm up, signaling reservations. "That's really your choice, Dan. But most reasonable people say it can't hurt, with a good doctor in charge. I think a lot more people would get that kind of help, if they could afford it."

"And we can?"

"Absolutely. Don't worry about it."

"You make it sound pretty simple."

"It's really the doctor's problem, and if he's any good, he or she can handle it."

"I'm in," said Danny, closing the deal.

During drinks before dinner, while Danny began his homework upstairs, the elders reported their joint assessment to Dorothy: the boy was OK, probably would avoid hurting anybody else at school, and would tell her or one of them if he needed help. As to his father, Danny was, and seemed likely to remain, bitter. He adored his mother. If he felt he or she needed help, he was likely to tell the grandfathers to make sure it came through. But it would probably be prudent to keep Gary away from his son, as much as the court would allow, and be alert for trouble if they did meet. Despite Gary's size and weight advantage, twelve-year-old Danny could probably put his father in the hospital with his bare hands.

The two men stayed on for ten days and enjoyed their time bonding with Danny and backing up Dorothy. They supported her objectives on the critical issues she had prioritized and helped revive her spirits and get her looking forward to a new life. They also left no doubts that they would return on a moment's notice.

DANNY '90 VI

AFTER A BIT MORE RITUAL, MOYNIHAN, LIKE THE REIGNING CHAMP ducking through the ropes, shrugging off his robe into his seconds' arms, pounding his gloves together and giving his opponent a rueful nod that says let's get it on, strode to the space between the bench and the jury box, nodded respectfully to both, and started his opening with "Your Honor, if it please the Court . . ."

I had almost $500,000 in hard earned cash and marketable securities to my name at last count, and it flashed through my mind that I would have given every cent of that to be in Phil's shoes as he laid out his case with appropriate emphasis, care, and effect. There was not a competing sound in the courtroom until he had finished telling the jury how he would prove that the brilliant, astoundingly successful, handsome young man in the dock was a master criminal conducting his vast illegal financial schemes on a scale probably as great as any other private citizen in history had ever conceived or attempted.

And then, after still more ritual, the witness parade began. None of the counties I had heard from reported in. But one after another, well spoken, clearly educated and financially savvy, relatively young MBAs, lawyers, and PhDs in mathematics, computer science, chemistry, sociology, government, epidemiology, materials science, economics, behavioral science, linguistics, and related disciplines were "led," despite my frequent objections, through the stories of how they had been hired by Daniel Miller and/or his senior minions to find specifically sought and randomly encountered bits of special information, largely unknown to investors and traders, large and small, which might, and frequently did, affect the market value of the securities of hundreds of public companies around the world.

Each was asked to describe the particular manner in which he or she was compensated for providing Miller the "confidential" information they found and delivered to him, and the range of methods utilized to provide such compensation was as dazzling as the scope of the information itself.

Several of the witnesses said they believed Miller's ability to process and recognize the implications of information was almost, or more frequently, "veritably," or "absolutely," superhuman. One MIT postdoctoral researcher and lecturer in computer science, an attractive woman in her late twenties, said that Miller's ability to comprehend the most abstruse subtleties of conceptual breakthroughs in her discipline was beyond anything she had encountered in the highest rated creative minds among the faculty at MIT.

An associate professor of mathematics at the Columbia School of Graduate Studies said that Miller sent in three members of his own staff to help prove the young scholar's overarching variant on the Theory of Large Numbers. The three Miller people then assisted him, designated as the principal researcher, in writing a major paper on his theory and the proof which he understood was the lynchpin of his MacArthur grant.

Others told of Miller's sending informants to Las Vegas, Monte Carlo, and Macao, on instruction to back their casino play with apparently unlimited funds until their luck reverted to the mean, and of buying stock in the name of checkable offshore entities and holding positions just long enough to liquidate the accounts and place the proceeds in vaults and numbered accounts at compliant banks throughout the world.

Every witness identified Danny. Every witness denied making an explicit deal with the prosecution. Some said they had indeed placed faith in general assurances of "recommendations" in return for cooperation, but received no firm commitments of leniency. Several said they had simply become so disgusted with Danny's manipulation of people and markets that they had come forward voluntarily to help bring him down. I tuned out. But as I observed them, it didn't appear to me that the jurors did.

On a lunch break midway through the parade, Miller and McGuiness suggested he would consider a plea.

"Just what kind of a plea did you have in mind," I asked.

"The least they'll take," Miller said.

"I see," I said. Then I turned to Farkas. "What's your opinion, Judge?"

"What is yours, Peter? You certainly know the prosecutors' thinking."

I sat back and let the tension build for a few minutes, closing my eyes as if to think harder. Then I said, "I doubt if they'll do any deal with you, Danny. But if they'd even consider it, I think they'd demand full restitution, as they calculate it, whatever is enough to clean you out. And at least ten years in a federal penitentiary.

"And when we go back in, I think we're going to hear about flight risk rendering bail impossible, given the amount of money you have and where it might be by now."

"I'm not exactly a thrill killer," Danny said.

"No, but they think you're more dangerous," I replied.

"That's patently absurd," he said.

McGuiness, apparently dazed, hadn't said a word.

"If there is any crime whatsoever here, and I do not concede that for a minute, it is classically victimless," Danny added.

"In your view, perhaps, Danny. But I can assure you that certainly is not the way the U.S. Attorney sees it," I said.

"Who's the victim? Show me a single one."

"Well, Miller," the judge said, "just arguendo, from their point of view, the entire financial system of the industrialized world is your victim. It is, after all, based on trust and the acceptance of a certain amount of fair dealing. At least that's what some of your colleagues and their defenders tell us.

"But with you on the loose, sir, that's out the window. Any sucker buying chips at your casino would have a better shot with Russian Imperials. Market manipulators and Inside Information Operators don't get too big to fail. They get busted and sent up, and like old soldiers, they just fade away."

He didn't even appear to be saying it vindictively, although I was damn sure he was, given his stake in the case. But he went on. "I've tried to answer your questions to the best of my ability. Now, I'd appreciate it if you'd answer one of mine."

"Try me," Danny said.

"Since you obviously knew all of those witnesses and what they could testify to, what was the point in playing those ridiculous games with us, stripping us of any chance of giving you an effective defense? Not that I think that in the face of that overwhelming evidence of massive criminality, we could have won for you, or even significantly mitigated your guilt, but if you had leveled with us, we could at least have contrived something that made you look less like Public Enemy Number One and us a little less like incompetent lawyers. What was your point?"

Danny folded his hands together on the table in front of him, looked at them with a little sardonic smile on his lips, and then up at both of us to answer.

"Well, Your Honor . . . ," he began.

But the judge interrupted him. "There's no reason to use that honorific anymore, Miller. I'm not a judge now."

"Then why do you have everybody address you as Judge?"

"It's just a gesture of respect, not at my instance."

"Whatever you say, Judge."

At that moment, I'd had enough. I stood up from the table, informed the judge, respectfully, that I thought I had better return to the courtroom and review my notes, never looking at Miller, and when Farkas nodded, I walked out of the restaurant. So the rest of this account I've reconstructed from what he told me later that day.

"I'd still like to hear your answer," he said as I was leaving. "What reason could you possibly have for acting in a manner so destructive to your own interests?"

Danny leaned in with a sort of demonic smile. "Of course, you know what my real interests are."

"Miller, since I think you're not wholly rational, indeed, far from it, I wouldn't presume to guess."

Miller replied, "So let's get right to the point, eh?"

Farkas, "Right to it, if there is any."

"I didn't just pick Peter out of the alumni directory, Judge."

"Given your well documented appetite for useful information, let's assume so."

"I did my due diligence, as usual."

"Due or undue, an arguable distinction in your case, let us assume you did some investigating."

"You bet your self-righteous ass I did, Judge."

"And found?"

"That Peter came to your firm because you personally wanted him there."

"Ten out of ten, Miller. You're brilliant. I'm the lead partner and the principal rainmaker. I like and respect Peter Cowen, whom I've known all his life, and I can see him as my natural successor, just young enough to be patient about it and superbly qualified by talent and character. And, incidentally, the son of my best friend since childhood. How in the world could you have figured that out? It's absolute sorcery, Miller. No wonder you've been so successful."

"The point is, Judge, I did get the facts, and I put them together correctly."

"Brilliant, Holmes. Absolutely brilliant."

"And I took it a step further."

"Ah," said the judge, "now it gets truly interesting."

"I realized you were two insufferably self-righteous peas in a pod, you and your protégé, Peter."

"I have been called worse with less cause."

"But not Peter Cowen, Judge. He gets an unqualified good press. Particularly for a fellow of his limited ability."

"And why does that matter to you?"

"Because he's a sanctimonious prig, and I find it very irritating that he's become a person of importance by sucking up to you."

The judge was now looking much more closely at Danny, as if seeing something he had previously missed. "And I completely misread you."

"All the way," said Miller.

"You never wanted us to win for you."

"You never stood a chance."

"Because you knew you never stood a chance."

"That depends on what you consider winning."

"Embarrassing us is winning?"

"That's a definitional issue. I'd say derailing Peter and taking his godfather down a few pegs adds up to a pretty satisfying result for me."

"And you're still going to feel that way when you've lost your fortune and you're locked up in a federal penitentiary?"

"If that's what happens."

"How can it not?"

"That's my business, not yours."

"I've got another question for you."

"We're not due back in the courtroom for another half hour. Try me. I'll answer if I want to."

"When you knew they were going to come after you, why didn't you leave the country and go visit your offshore money?"

"And leave this unfinished business behind?"

"This business of losing your fortune and going to prison?"

"The business of seeing justice done."

"To whom?"

"Cowen and you, of course."

"Miller, I'm just beginning to realize you are insane."

"That's certainly the way it looks, doesn't it?"

"My God, is that your game plan?"

"I'm afraid you'll have to wait and see, Judge."

"You've made arrangements to have yourself declared insane and a conservator appointed to take over your assets. Then you'd stage a miraculous 'recovery' under psychiatric treatment? That's it, isn't it?"

"And that strikes you as a miscarriage of justice, because I'm not really insane at all."

"I wouldn't say that. No sane man would place himself in that kind of jeopardy to settle some petty, adolescent disagreement."

"Life is risk, Farkas. I hedge mine rather adroitly. And I'm in no real danger, I assure you."

"Maybe, if you could ever pull it off, but there's not a chance in a million. It's impossible."

"Possibly, but then again, maybe that's not my play. Maybe I've got some other ideas. You'll just have to wait and see."

"All this to what end, Miller? To damage Peter Cowen? To blight his career and his life? What in the name of God did he do to you to warrant this madman's retribution?"

"I very much doubt that a man like you, with your tidy little mind and your belief in justice as symmetry, would ever understand."

"Try me."

"Well, for starters, he was always so unbearably self-righteous."

"An unpleasant characteristic, but hardly unforgiveable."

"That's up to the victim."

"OK. Let's accept that for the moment."

"And he practically dared me to take away the girl he loved."

"Foolish, perhaps. Hardly offensive in itself. And did you take the dare?"

"The first chance I had with her. I took her in a very brutal manner and degraded her in every way I could think of. I made a little sex slave of her, and she loved it. She hated herself, but she loved it and she loved me, slavishly."

"And did Peter ever learn about this?"

"Of course. I insisted she tell him every punishing, penetrating detail."

"And what did Peter do?"

"First, he covered his ears and told her he didn't want to hear about it. But I had warned her about that. And I had made her go to him naked under a raincoat to make the confession and take the raincoat off to show him the marks and act out the movements, because I knew he wouldn't have the guts to throw her out of his room naked. She did exactly as she was told, and he did exactly as I predicted, both of them sucking up the abuse like cocaine."

"And that's all Peter did?"

"No. He left her in his room, sobbing in the fetal position, on the little Nantucket hooked rug he had between his bed and his desk, and came looking for me, in the gym, where I'd told her to tell him I would be."

"And?"

"He found me in the wrestling room and made a run at me, and I beat the shit out of him. I worked him over pretty well and broke his right wrist for good measure, just to keep him out of basketball for a full season. He's a quick healer, though, and he was back in shape for the tennis season, still playing just a little better than I was and hanging on at number 1."

"That must have been deeply disappointing to you."

"Spare me the sarcasm, old man. You asked for this."

"That's right," the judge admitted, "and I got what I deserved."

"That's not all," Danny said.

"It's all I want to hear."

"But you're going to hear a little more."

"Suit yourself. I don't have a gavel here. If I did I'd probably throw it right at your head, you little monster."

"She still believes that creep is a better man than I am. My own fucking wife, and she says he's the real man, and she'll always love him. I'm just a sickness she caught and hasn't gotten over yet. Would you believe that, that pumped-up Eagle Scout a better man than I am?"

"By a country mile, Miller. It's not even close. But my partner's gone back to the courtroom, and we'd better get over there, too. There's more *undermenschen* work to do, and I'm quite sure the judge won't let us resign the case at this stage."

DANNY '90 VII

I had never met Max Landers before, but Danny had mentioned him in our early days together, referring to him as his "extra" grandfather and with, for Danny, a good deal of respect, which I had attributed to his apparently considerable wealth. I made no effort to check him out before I OK'd the appointment, because his secretary had clearly identified him and herself to my assistant, so what was the point? I was sure he wanted to talk about Danny, and there was no way I could refuse.

I went out to reception to greet him, and we shook hands there before walking back to my office together. I offered him the couch, and he, politely, in an elegant, beautifully modulated, nearly U Brit voice, asked if I'd mind his taking a straight-backed chair, citing "a bit of discomfort" from the flight in, earlier that afternoon. But he was about as fit an older man as I'd ever seen, exquisitely poised and immediately ingratiating.

He said that Dorothy had the most delightful things to say about me and sent her very best regards. I thanked him, offered him some refreshment, which he declined, and he smoothly got right to his point.

"I have a rather unusual mix of friends and contacts, not all your everyday clubmen," he said. "And some of them have some even more 'exotic' friends, in places high and low. I, therefore, have a good deal of confidence, for reasons with which I need not burden you, that my natural grandson will not suffer any physical abuse in prison. But I do think that once he fully realizes that the rejection of his insanity plea is irreversible, no matter what kind of act he puts

207

on, and he is really going to spend many of the best years of his life behind bars, he may, in fact, go mad.

"What's more, and perhaps the most troubling concern of all, is that having marked himself a faker, he will be the boy who cried wolf too often and wins nothing but additional years added to his sentence for disruptive behavior.

"I am here to ask you if you believe you have enough influence with him to persuade him not to let himself drift into real madness, or be perceived to have done so. He is still very young. He is brilliant and talented in many areas. If he devotes his wits and his talents to something constructive for all the years he will be forced to spend in prison, he can come out well before he is fifty, a better man, with a good life ahead of him."

"Sir," I said, "it grieves me to have to tell you I have absolutely no influence over him. I agree with your prescription, but I am the last man to choose to give it to him. My support would condemn it."

"He is that far gone?"

"Quite. I'm certain."

"Is it the loss of his fortune?"

"More the loss of the game."

"Because his inheritance from me alone will make him rich, and his other grandfathers are extremely wealthy men. He should know that."

"I'm sure he does," I said. "Danny really does understand money, Mr. Landers."

"If he stays sane, Peter. I hope you don't mind my calling you Peter. I feel very close to you, even though we've never met before. As I said, he knows very well about the family money. If he indeed is, and remains, in possession of his wits. And that's the very large *if*, isn't it?"

"Yes, sir."

"I have the sense that Danny hasn't behaved very well toward you, Peter. I'm sorry."

"That really doesn't matter any more, Mr. Landers. If I could help him, I would, after everything. But I know I can't. I'm sorry."

"Well, I believe you, Peter. And I'm grateful for both your time and your candor. If there is anything I could do to redress whatever Danny did or didn't do to disappoint you, you have only to let me know. Then consider it done, whatever it might be."

"I thank you, sir. I'm only sorry I can't help you or Danny."

"You're a good man, Peter. You move on, don't you? It's a pity Danny did not heed your example or your advice."

"You're very kind, sir. I hope you know I wish he had."

We shook hands. I escorted him back to the lobby and said good-bye. I watched him walk sturdily into the elevator, and then headed back to my office to clean up some work.

Danny's appeal on the grounds of attorneys' incompetence was filed by McGuiness's firm and attracted some publicity which stung. Then his third firm, a good deal lower in professional standing but notoriously hard-nosed, filed a civil malpractice suit against us in the State Supreme Court, and we had to battle with our insurers when they insisted we settle it. But we were still refusing to settle, despite threats by the insurer to cancel our coverage going forward and weekly intramural "debates" among the partners when the appeal was denied and our insurers dropped their demand that we settle the malpractice suit. Those results did not immediately restore my standing in the firm or the profession, but my partners forgave, if they did not forget. Between Farkas and Milan, I had some formidable allies; both the firm and I climbed back.

DANNY '90 VIII

We followed them to the Vanderbilt Avenue entrance. One of the three bulky men stayed in the car while the other two came out with Danny between them. We left the driver in ours and caught up with them just as they were entering the station. We went down the broad staircase, and then turned immediately onto the stairs down to the lower terminal. They were moving quickly. But we had to keep a pace that Glenn could manage and the distance between the two groups widened.

I kept looking to see what kind of hold they had on Danny and realized they weren't restraining him at all. He just walked along between them. We picked up our pace on the straightaway and got to the track entrance right behind them. As they started down the ramp, one of them turned and said pleasantly, "We'll give you some time to say good-bye when we get to the car we want."

We walked along just a step apart until they reached the middle of the train and stopped. The one who had talked to me said something softly to Danny, and then the two of them walked away from him. One of them took up a position fifteen feet further down the platform, and the other walked back behind us about the same distance.

Danny turned to us, hands in his topcoat pockets, and said, evenly, "Well, I guess this is where the story ends."

There was a pause, and then I answered, "Not necessarily the story, Danny. Just a chapter."

"Yeah," he smiled.

Julie moved up and put her arms around him, her head bowing into the crick of his neck. I could see her straining to hold him as tightly as she could. "Oh, Danny, be smart up there.

"Take care of yourself, will you?" she asked urgently. He raised his arms to embrace her and kissed her lightly on the top of her head.

"I always do, don't I?" Danny answered, still holding her as she clutched him.

"I don't know, Daniel," she said, suppressing her sobs. "I always thought you did, but now I don't know," she said, almost keening. "You have to try, use all of your wits to try. It's so terribly dangerous."

"Max has my back, Julie. Believe me, he's told me. And he's always good for his word. I'm his blood, Julie, for better or for worse, and he has connections, even there. So don't you worry. I'll be all right. He won't let me down."

Glenn walked up to them, with his arms outstretched, an exceptionally graceful man, in an elegant Astrakhan coat, moving awkwardly. Danny disengaged himself from Julie and took his adoptive grandfather's right hand in his. Then he looked around for Max, who was not anywhere in sight.

"I've never been much good at this kind of thing," Glenn said.

"Have you ever had much practice?" Danny chided. "But then, maybe you and Grandpa Max have had your share during the war."

"I didn't mean the prison part," Glenn said, almost in a whisper. There were tears in his eyes.

"I know, Grandpa, don't worry. I just never could resist putting you on."

"That's OK."

Danny turned to me. "There's something I would like to ask you to do, Peter," he said.

"Sure."

"Give my mother a call or drop by once in a while. She won't be going out much for some time."

"Count on it."

"I will."

The conductor called the train, and the detectives said they had to go. I took Danny's hand, feeling a little pressure behind the eyes myself. Julie embraced him again. Glenn stood by.

The marshals and Danny entered the train and found seats, one fed next to Danny, the other across the aisle. We waited a few minutes, last call, and then the train was moving. Danny looked back through the window once, nodded, and then turned his head forward.

We walked back through the platform at Glenn's pace, up the two flights of stairs and out onto Vanderbilt. When we got to the waiting car where the driver was holding the right rear door open, Glenn put his big hands on my shoulders and said, "You did what you could, Peter, and we thank you."

"Really my job, sir," I said. "No thanks necessary."

Julie and he kissed; he and I shook hands.

"Can I drop you somewhere?" he asked. I looked at Julie briefly, and then told him we would walk a bit.

The wind was cold and damp on Vanderbilt as we headed uptown. But we were both well bundled up and gloved, Julie with a long woolen scarf that she twisted about her head. It was white wool, and from a distance looked like a wound dressing.

"Do you understand?" she asked as we walked.

"Some of it."

"I don't. Unless it's just that he never could tolerate losing."

"Or not winning. But it's much more complicated than that, I think."

She stopped walking, turned, reached for me to hold her, and began to sob against my chest as I put my arms around her.